A Wenceslas Christmas

BOOKS BY SHIRLEY BURTON

HISTORICAL FICTION
Homage: Chronicles of a Habitant

THRILLERS
Don't Open the Door
Red Jackal
THOMAS YORK SERIES:
Under the Ashes - Book One
The Frizon - Book Two
Rogue Courier - Book Three
Secret Cache - Book Four
The Paris Network - Book Five
The Masquerade - Book Six

MYSTERY
Epitaph of an Imposter
Sentinel in the Moors
INSPECTOR FURNACE MYSTERIES:
Mystery at Grey Stokes
Swindle: Mystery at Sea

CHRISTMAS
Clockmaker's Christmas
Christmas Treasure Box
A Wenceslas Christmas
The Wish Store

FANTASY
Boy from Saint-Malo

shirleyburtonbooks.com

A Wenceslas Christmas

Shirley Burton

HIGH STREET PRESS

HIGH STREET PRESS
Niagara-on-the-Lake, ON, Canada
highstreetpress.com
shirleyburtonbooks.com
First printing 2020

This book is a work of fiction. Names, characters, places, and incidents are the product of the author's imagination or are used fictitiously. Any resemblance to actual events, locales or persons, living or dead, is entirely coincidental.

A WENCESLAS CHRISTMAS Copyright © 2020 Shirley Burton. All rights reserved. This book may not be reproduced in any form without permission.

Printed in the United States of America, Canada, UK, Australia, and global distribution in Europe, Asia, and South America.
Available in paperback, hardcover, and eBook formats.
Cover photo licensed Shutterstock.com.
Design and edit: Bruce Burton

Library and Archives Canada Cataloguing in Publication.

Burton, Shirley, 1950-, author
    A Wenceslas Christmas/ Shirley Burton

Issued in print and electronic versions.
ISBN 978-1-927839-30-3 (pbk.). —ISBN 978-1-927839-31-7 (hardcover)
ISBN 978-1-927839-32-4 (ebook)

*"Oh an Austrian went yodeling on a mountain so high,
When along came an avalanche interrupting his cry!
Yo-delayy, keee."*

CONTENTS

1	Three Weeks before Christmas	1
2	The Protégé	12
3	Avalanche Rescue	21
4	Grand Introductions	27
5	The Chef Exchange	36
6	Departure to Paris	44
7	Logan's Foothold	53
8	Retrospect of a Tragedy	61
9	The Boucher Markets	69
10	The Food Critic	78
11	Marceau in Paris	86
12	Secrets of the Great Book	93
13	The Bequest	101
14	Good King Wenceslas	107
15	Logan's Plea	112
16	Woodcutter's Cabin	119
17	True Meaning of Christmas	128
18	A Joyful Feast	134
19	Taking Goodwill to Chamonix	141
20	The Contestant, Chef Marceau	146
21	The Proposal	152
22	Flaxie's Inheritance	162
23	Cards on the Table	167
24	New Year's Eve	174
25	Logan Goes Missing	179
26	Recovered Plans	186
27	Stanhope Connection	192
28	Lost is Found	200
29	The Promise	205

1

Three weeks before Christmas
Mont Blanc in the French Alps

Bells jingled and jangled as teams of stately Clydesdales tromped through the cobbled streets of Chamonix, shuttling skiers and tourists from hotels to the ski buses.

Light-hearted exuberance filled the air as Christmas carols piped from the decorated shops. At Place du Mont Blanc, the town square, the rotating arms of a giant plaster statue of a snowman waved up and down to a record of 'Frosty the Snowman' that blared over the crowd.

Below him, mascots of the jolly snowman with coal-black buttons and red scarves and sashes zigzagged on the main thoroughfare posing for pictures.

Around the circumference, a miniature train overflowing with elves puffed toward a workshop, passing an alpine minstrel group that was performing 'An Austrian Went Yodeling' with their most imaginative wiggling actions and yodels.

Magically, the town had transformed into the North Pole in its annual tradition, with gondolas gliding high above the mountains, and trains meandering through the rocky ridges, stopping at charming villages along the route.

Twice a day, the merchant van's jalopy horn sounded and unloaded beautifully gift-wrapped parcels to hotel concierge desks.

Above Chamonix, Mont Blanc's chalets and lodges were crested on a landing accessible by a funicular and cog tram or a rugged winding road.

The most historic and elegant hotel was the Grand Marceau. The inn was solidly booked with a cheerful hustle and bustle filling the lobby. Porters scurried about with racks and carts dodging the queues of line-ups at reception.

The historic décor of the grand hall was festooned in Renaissance art, great wall tapestries, and delicately carved King Louis XIV cabinets, overstuffed sofas, and chairs. On the arrival of the Christmas season, decorated trees were stationed throughout in a magical atmosphere with carols played from the early morning.

High on the mountains above them, a fresh white blanket of snow glittered in the sunlight. But the locals knew that the beast was breathing, waiting for the moment to purge its winter weight, to awaken from sleep, and consume the unsuspecting.

Today was December 4th, and the revered Bernard Marceau sat in his office behind the culinary work area. Swinging his chair around, he stared at the calendar. For his sixty years, he was spry and slightly rotund with a well-coiffed, white beard enhancing his square jaw and polished rosy cheeks.

He was born and raised at the Grand Marceau. From a

young age, he was enchanted by the workings and assembly of the kitchens, following his father wherever he went. He never thought of any future that didn't include the hotel and the career of a chef, and he'd applied himself to culinary training, becoming self-taught in five languages.

He tossed the letter back onto his desk.

Such an honor and privilege to be invited, yet I cannot see my way to leave Flaxie at such a busy time. The hotel is fully booked, taxing every staff member.

The Grand Marceau lands were granted by King Louis XV of France, the Marquis de Marceau. For hundreds of years, royalty was entertained in private suites with turrets and the fantastic alpine and glacier views. Regal columns encased the grand entrance and majestic balconies offered impeccable panoramas of the French Alps.

The Marceau, years before, achieved its first Michelin star earned by its famed chef, Bernard Marceau. Although the hotel did not share a city populace, it sat above Chamonix on more than a hundred acres of rolling hills, accessible by a cog tram, shuttle buses, and snow caterpillars.

The magnificent historic stone edifice stood with four stories of guest rooms and another floor above for penthouse apartments and royal suites. As the demand for facilities grew, an elegant dining room was built on a terrace overlooking the valley, to provide a romantic vista.

At Christmas, it was even more enchanting with a forest line of trees lit in crimson, emerald, sapphire blue, and golden amber lights welcoming tourists to this wonderland.

Again, Marceau picked up the fine embossed parchment and reread it.

Monsieur Marceau,

It would be our honor to invite the esteemed Chef Bernard Marceau as a participant at the international gastronomic chef competition at the King George hotel in Paris this Christmas. We are delighted to inform you that you have been nominated by a prestigious committee of international culinary experts as one of Europe's foremost chefs du cuisine.

First-class accommodations have been held for you from December 9th to the 29th to be at our distinguished hotel with a designated sous-chef personally assigned to you.

As discussed in our telephone interview, we understand that your resort may be inconvenienced by your absence over the holidays and we have taken the liberty of recruiting a renowned sous-chef from the King George to take your place while you are in Paris.

Please call my direct line anytime, Bernard. Otherwise, a limousine will arrive for you in Mont Blanc on the morning of the 9th to transport you to Paris.

Signed: Monsieur Gaspard Morningside, Esq., Senior Director, The King George Hotel of France.

A familiar shadow appeared outside the glass door, followed by a soft rap.

"Come in, Ingrid."

Leaning against the door frame with her head tilted, she subtly asked, "Bernard you have to tell her. She's more capable than you realize."

"You know about the competition?" He gave a half-smile knowing that, of course, Ingrid watched over him every day.

"Of course, Bernard, I've lived in this hotel for the last twenty years—we're family, and a family doesn't keep secrets. We're here for each other to offer encouragement when an opportunity comes along."

Ingrid paused and searched Marceau's eyes. "Dearest, Bernard, you've watched over Flaxie for the last seventeen years, but she's a grown woman now. Don't you see that she

A Wenceslas Christmas 5

follows in your footsteps with adoration? She is so much like you were, revering your father."

"But we're in our busiest time of the year and I've never left Flaxie at Christmas."

"We will be so busy, there won't be time for regret."

"Ingrid, what would I do without you?"

"I don't intend that you'll ever have to find out."

Bernard looked upon her for a moment as a stranger.

I've not paid attention to my Ingrid, the lovely fair maiden from Austria that walked with a satchel in hand up the hillside from the village demanding that my father hire her. She is as beautiful as the day I first laid eyes on her. Yes, I have taken her for granted.

"It's been twenty years, Ingrid. You were here the night of the tragedy at Grenoble when Flaxie's parents were taken. You've been a substitute mother to Flaxie and my dearest friend in all the world. I don't know how I would have gotten through the rough times without you. I should have paid more attention."

"All I ask, Bernard, is that you give me a dance at the New Year's Eve gala when you return." She felt an awkward blush flood her cheeks then remembered why she had arrived at his door.

"Bernard, Monsieur Willoughby has been calling again from Paris. He heard of the possibility of you being in the city and is demanding a meeting. He said it was very important and time is running out."

Taking a few steps backward, she turned and swished away.

Yes, yes, Willoughby, I can't put that off much longer.

Reaching for his white monogrammed chef's jacket, Bernard marched to the front lobby, swinging his arms for momentum. The letter was folded in his breast pocket.

"Roberto! Monsieur Dion, I'd like a word."

"Of course, Monsieur Marceau."

"First of all, have you seen Flaxie?"

"Ah oui, she is seeing a ski group to their rooms. She'll be back in a few minutes. Can I help?" Roberto was eager to be of service. Jovial and twice married in his early forties, he held dual French-Italian citizenship.

Bernard made a shoulder check for privacy then lowered his voice to a whisper. "I'd like your opinion, Roberto. Do you think you and Flaxie can carry on?"

Taking the outstretched parchment, Roberto carefully read the document from the King George. His eyes widened showing his pleasure.

"Ah, Monsieur Marceau, this is a great honor for you. Of course, we can carry on. We wish you much success at the competition and the international recognition you deserve among your peers."

Roberto turned, at a momentary distraction as a golden-haired, young woman in a festive, embroidered, winter-green dirndl dress flounced across the hall.

"Monsieur, Flaxie is coming."

Roberto returned the envelope and professed to busy himself at the reception counter, purposefully stationed within hearing range.

"My dear Uncle Bernard, it's so nice to see you this lovely day. Don't you adore this hustle and bustle? Everyone is so filled with anticipation."

Flaxie tucked her arm about his ample waist smiling in adoration, with her blue eyes twinkling.

"Ma chérie, may I have a word?" Marceau's face grew somber.

"Ah, this is serious then," she teased.

"You are a vision of your dear mother. She would be proud to see you now. My gosh . . . your birthday is coming up. Twenty-five years, where have they gone?"

Yes, her 25th is not far away, no wonder Willoughby is getting anxious.

"Your flattery is meant as a distraction, Uncle. You have something on your mind that you need to tell me."

Flaxie planted a hand on each side of his face and stared him directly in the eyes. Then she kissed each cheek.

"Read this letter from Monsieur Gaspard Morningside. He is from the King George in Paris. I don't know how else to start."

Bernard smoothed his jacket as she fidgeted to straighten it. Taking the parchment letter, she oohed at its prestige.

"Looks quite official, seal, and all." She let her hand run over the raised, embossed letterhead.

Bernard watched as Flaxie's eyes raced over each sentence until a broad smile broke the wait.

"This is wonderful, Uncle. You should have told me sooner. You have only a few days to prepare."

Flaxie spotted Roberto edging closer. "And Roberto and I will do the hotel justice in your absence, won't we Roberto?"

"It will be excellent, Monsieur Marceau. We will have a wonderful Christmas for our guests."

Flaxie immediately spun with ideas. "Well then, Uncle, let's start getting you ready. Your jackets and aprons must be stark white and crisp . . . and Roberto, send for the travel trunks from the storeroom."

In a sparse garret overlooking Montparnasse, Logan Powell gazed out of his windows at the glimmering beauty of the Eiffel Tower and the dazzling neon of Moulin Rouge. He thrived in the French culture and was enthralled with the rich historic heritage of Paris. In his spare time, he squeezed in walks to museums and strolled the cobbled streets with the joy of being a Parisian.

Ah, to live in the city of light and have an empty heart since Brigitte was taken. I have spent the last eight years of my life trying to achieve an unattainable dream. I have success as a sous-chef under the great Augustus here in Paris, but I want to have pride in my efforts. King George will continue to maintain their Michelin awards with or without me.

His hopes were heightened earlier that day when Monsieur Morningside came to him in the culinary workroom with a proposal. This was the second time the director had come to enquire of Logan.

"Monsieur Powell, I will make this brief and to the point. You have worked well under Chef Augustus these last few years but you must be aware there is always competition. Your training at Covent Market Academy in London is highly notable, as is your rise in the industry. You've come highly recommended for the post I am willing to present.

"Ah, to the point. Monsieur Bernard Marceau of Mont Blanc has been invited to Paris for the international gourmet conference. As you can appreciate, he cannot leave his fine establishment without a head chef. I have offered your services, and of course, you are free to take Marianne as your assistant if you wish.

"You will arrive at the Grand on the 8th for an introduction to Chef Marceau, then return to Paris for our New Year's Eve gala—it will be an extravaganza of who's who in Paris. I will require immediate consent to continue with arrangements."

Morningside's eyes bulged as they usually did, but today they exuded even more authority.

Logan stood in momentary, stunned silence. "Indeed, Sir,

it would be my great honor."

With that, Morningside turned on his heels and was gone without the opportunity for Logan's multiple queries that were rushing his mind.

The Grand Marceau is a coup to be sure, but will I be oriented by the master or arrive cold? How many kitchen staff do they have, what are their menus, do I take my menus, why will I need to have Marianne? Is my return here guaranteed?

Logan was a handsome, eligible bachelor simply because he had no time for romance. At thirty years of age, he'd had his share of match-making by well-meaning clients but he had focused on his career ambition toward head chef.

Chef Augustus had challenged his sous-chefs every day to present new and exciting entrées or appetizers vying for their placement on the menu.

But Logan's experience with his boss, Augustus, had soured with good reason.

During a past encounter with a Cannes seafood merchant at the morning market, Logan had acquired a choice shipment of abalone, cuttlefish, and oysters. Receiving accolades for a cuttlefish stuffed with scallops in a delicate prawn mousse drizzled with Szechuan pepper sauce on a bed of root puree, the feature was added to the upcoming festive menus with the credited addition, 'a la Logan'.

But to Logan's disappointment and dismay, he found an article in a culinary magazine where Chef Augustus had submitted the recipe under *his* signature and any mention of a la Logan had disappeared.

From that time on, instead of an advantage, tension grew between him and his head chef. It was apparent every time their eyes met, as both understood the consternation.

Raised in Brooklyn, New York, of Irish and English heritage, Logan Powell had set his sights on culinary schools in London, Rome, and Paris. A handsome man, he had a chiseled jaw with dreamy, sapphire-violet eyes and medium-brown curly hair with natural red highlights.

His only facial imperfection was a jagged scar at the square of his jaw below his left ear that he'd acquired years before in London when he successfully defended a friend from a mugger with a switchblade.

Late into the night, Logan searched the internet for anything he could find on Bernard Marceau, the Grand Hotel, Chamonix, and the staff and menus.

It became clear that the gourmet competition in Paris would begin on the 9th, thus only time for an introduction and a simple tour of the hotel's dining rooms and kitchens before Marceau would depart.

Picking up the phone at 2 a.m., he rang through to Marianne.

"Allo, Marianne. How do you feel about skiing in the French Alps over Christmas, all expenses paid?"

A groggy and disgruntled voice replied. "Logan, you are crazy. What are you talking about?"

Marianne had been a valued prep assistant working alongside Logan for the last two years at the George. Over time she could anticipate his needs without implicit instruction.

After an apology for the late hour, Logan explained his meeting with Morningside and the opportunity. Concealing his fear, he appeared frivolous with his description of magical terrain and luxury vacation.

"Are you in?"

"It seems I have already been assigned. What choice do I have?"

"None, I will make travel arrangements in the morning.

A Wenceslas Christmas

By the way, do you ski as we will be on the crest of the magnificent Mont Blanc?"

"I've lived in Paris most of my life. Of course, I don't ski. But there's always a time to give it a try. Bonsoir, Logan."

2

The Protégé

Gaspard Morningside allowed a travel day for the staff exchange to Mont Blanc.

Logan Powell and Marianne arrived at a small chalet in Chamonix late the night of the 7th with plans of an early morning ski outing on Mont Blanc. Logan wanted to burn off his nerves before the rendezvous at the Grand to begin his apprenticeship assignment.

"It is a marvelous hotel, Marianne. In high school, my parents sent me to Neuchâtel in Switzerland for several years. One weekend, a few of my friends gathered their resources and we came to Chamonix for an overnight at a chalet and we came up to the hotel for dinner.

"The food was incredible. I remember thinking how wonderful it would be to apprentice in such a marvelous establishment. Your experience here will be a true feather in your cap to, do you realize?"

A Wenceslas Christmas

"Logan, I am eager too for the morning but I'm more nervous about skiing. How good are you? Which slopes do you dare to try?"

"The black diamond would be invigorating but under the circumstances, it would be foolish to risk this opportunity. But I'm game for the mid-level chair lift."

"It seems, Logan, that I follow you like a blind sheep."

At Marianne's words, it only now occurred to him that he had taken her away from Paris at Christmas. Surely she had romantic plans that were waylaid.

"I have taken you away from Jean-Paul. I was so wrapped up in this honor and opportunity . . . and at Christmas no less. I didn't think of the consequences to you."

"Don't give it a thought. You know the saying 'absence makes the heart grow fonder'. Perhaps that will play to my advantage when I return New Year's Eve."

Logan winced to himself, wishing he'd shared her hopes of a loyal boyfriend but he'd seen Jean-Paul enough to know of his wandering eye.

Logan and Marianne booked into the first ski group for the next morning. From the shuttle between Chamonix to the chair lift at the base of Mont Blanc, they could see two distant helicopter groups descending from the black diamond. Lining up at the chair lift, they watched the first skiers gliding down the slopes.

The crispness of the overnight blanket was blinding to the eye and Marianne lowered her goggles to stop the glare.

"Good gracious, what ungodly hour were those skiers on the slopes? I haven't even had my first coffee of the day and look at me," Marianne teased as she advanced toward the chair lift, pushing her poles into fresh powder.

The operator, impatient with her hesitation, held the bar

up and gestured it was time.

"Come on, it's your turn. There's a lineup behind you," the young man urged. "Quickly, please."

Marianne reached for his hand and he pulled her on. Logan followed with adept skill and the chair rose quickly with their skis hanging in peril. The panorama was breathtaking as everything diminished into miniature size.

"The view is spectacular, Marianne. Over there see the glaciers and the Alps as if they extend to the end of the world!"

Marianne wrangled with the ski pole's wrist loop. "Logan, I'm not so sure I should be doing this."

"Watch the chairs ahead of us and follow what they do. I'll wait until you are off safely."

The three on the chair in front glided off with ease and continued down the slope giving Marianne a boost of confidence. Tightening her gloves, she gripped her poles for the leap off the chairlift.

"Alright, I'm ready."

Bernard Marceau was preoccupied like a mother hen preparing to leave the roost. Anxiety was building among the prep and serving staff as he micromanaged every detail, ensuring that every order had been placed and menus scrutinized. He continued a reserved but persistent rant.

"The protégé should be arriving today. Magnon, make sure all the supplies are ordered. Don't forget the truffles *must* be fresh from Provence. Cobb, send someone into Chamonix to hire more servers—go to Argentière or other villages until you find trained hires, the cream of the crop, and I'll pay bonuses accordingly."

The only person able to calm him was Ingrid. She knew he needed latitude to work through his concerns, but stayed near.

It was still dark and the first light hadn't come up over the mountains, but the clatter in the kitchen alerted Ingrid to Bernard's morning rustling.

Once Flaxie had reached her teen years and no longer needed a nanny, Ingrid's preferred choice in accommodation was in the staff quarters over the larder. With golden braids pinned atop her head and a chenille robe wrapped around her, Ingrid pushed open the revolving door on her way to find Bernard. The kitchen and prep areas were ablaze in light.

There he was poring over the great livre. It had been passed down from Bernard's father, and his grandfather before that.

The leather volume was fat with recipes, directions, lists of ingredients and where to find them, and names and phone numbers of suppliers. All the sketches and recipes were held together with an ancient deerskin belt.

The yellowed envelope from Willoughby & Singleton peeked out from the back cover and he shoved it back into its place.

Yes, the time has come, perhaps I will find the time while I'm in Paris.

With hands on her hips, Ingrid addressed him with a scold. "Bernard Marceau, leave the rest to the protégé. Everyone deserves a fair chance. You've been given this wonderful respect, now give the poor apprentice his opportunity and leave well enough alone.

"If you cannot sleep, that is another matter. I will make some nice espresso and we will watch the sun come up over Mont Blanc, but the kitchen is now off-limits to you."

"Ingrid, dearest, you don't understand."

"I do understand—that is why I am standing here."

Flaxie arose feeling disturbed but wasn't able to pinpoint her source of distress, whether bad dreams or perhaps sound and apprehension. It was December 8th, the day the sous-chef would arrive. But that was not what haunted her.

Looking out her window, she could still see the lights of the ski trail on Mont Blanc. The bonfires were being fed and the grooming cats were starting up the lower routes. Although the lifts were a distance away, she could hear the gears of the chairlift clicking and heaving as they always did.

"Why are the lights flickering? It's eerily calm. The sun will soon breach the horizon and the first group will make their way up the black diamond. The alpine shuttle will be here and we have two large groups signed up for the early bird. Although they forecast a beautiful sunny day, in my gut I hear a strange sound."

Feeling hungry, she made her way to the lobby where Roberto had laid out his usual pastries, juice, and coffee for the early risers. Taking the grand staircase from the third floor, she glided down to the foyer.

"Good morning, Roberto. Have you seen Uncle Bernard?"

Smiling with mild amusement, he replied. "They are both asleep in the back sunroom. Looks like they got up early and had coffee, but gave in to the fatigue of the excitement of the day."

Looking at her watch, she gasped. "Look at the time, it's 5:30 and the first breakfast seating is in an hour, Uncle will be in a tizzy to be late for his last breakfast here."

Flaxie rushed toward the kitchen to awaken Bernard. Instead, she ran into him full force. His cheeks were rosy with his usual jovial smile.

"Good morning, Flaxie, indeed you seem anxious to see

me."

"I hear you've been up for a while."

"I was, but thank goodness dear Ingrid came and rescued me. I had a marvelous espresso with my lovely friend on the terrace. But I see I'm needed for the breakfast specialties." He unfolded a fresh apron and hurried to his omelet pans.

"What can I do to help, Uncle?"

"Whatever you normally do this time of the morning. It is only another day, no different from yesterday or tomorrow."

The hotel was fully booked and dazzled in the pre-dawn darkness with a display of colored lights twisted around the pillars and trees in the outer courtyard. The valets wore red jackets with tails and top hats, pinned with boutonnières of golden bells on sprigs of evergreen.

The outer porch was lined with skis and boot racks under the auspice of the most particular German guide, Hans Brockmeier. Ski equipment was never allowed past the grand entrance, with every item logged, ticketed, signed for, and valeted, then kept under lock and key.

A convoy of jingling horse teams leading carriages and wagons was being driven up from the lower barns to be prepared for the shuttling.

Wearing a red down parka with an embroidered hotel crest, Flaxie stepped to the outer lobby to check in with Hans as she did every morning.

"Ah . . . it smells like Christmas."

She sniffed the fresh hay bales as the wagons passed. "Hans, do you hear something peculiar this morning?"

"Every morning the ski choppers make their drops at the peak of Mont Blanc right on cue at first dawn. Was that it? Some folks would pay dearly to be the first to see the sunrise.

I've gotten used to that sound and I don't pay any heed."

"Perhaps that is it. I was thinking of something different, like a rumbling or groaning . . . the mountain has a soul of its own and it's trying to say something."

Hans turned his head as if to listen for an interruption to the alpine silence.

"No, the ranger has predicated a bright, sunny day with a low-level avalanche warning."

Flaxie adjusted her woolen scarf and stared up the mountain. The hills were powdery-white and not yet crowded, allowing novice skiers to make fresh tracks on the uncrowded run.

Logan passed Marianne on the top of the slope and turned to see where she was. At that moment a cloud of white snow erupted over the peak and a sickening feeling hit him.

The first queue of skiers descended, then a second and a third. Marianne's body stiffened. "I feel the mountain heaving under my feet."

From the apex, the thunderous groaning roared, and up to the peak, the fracture widened in slow motion. Voices echoed across the mountain as an enormous rupture spewed ice and snow into the air surging an assault on the ski runs.

"Avalanche!"

Sirens and whistles blared as furrows of snow plowed down the mountain sweeping up everything in sight.

Hunter Bodine, the lead ranger, arrived within minutes on a snowmobile from the depot north of the village. Rescuers and searchers were already streaming up the cog and hiking trail from Chamonix, the response whenever sirens sounded.

As snow cat groomers and all-terrain vehicles were

A Wenceslas Christmas 19

dispatched to pick up lower slope skiers, the Bernese search dogs and sleds were assembled with partners to seek out beacons and signs of life.

The distant roar reached Bernard Marceau in his office. Devastated, he went to confer with Bodine.

"This is terrible. I cannot leave under these circumstances."

Bodine was in the laneway of the hotel portico where he had set up an outdoor command post. The avalanche disaster plan had been rehearsed many times, and everyone knew his responsibilities. The rescue was in gear like a well-oiled machine.

"Bonjour, Monsieur Marceau, c'est tragique but we have the best searchers. Unfortunately, protocol forbids me from dispatching rescuers until the snow has settled and the rumbling has ceased. The usual snowmobile patrols are already out there and we don't know their status. They are highly skilled and know where to seek shelter."

"I understand, Hunter. Take whatever you need from the hotel. Feel free to assemble in the conference room on the main floor near the ballroom. I'll send for coffee urns and croissants."

For what seemed an eternity, Bernard and Flaxie watched and waited for the siren to signal the rescue's start.

"Hans told me we sent out a full bus with fifteen skiers before the avalanche. Hopefully, they were too early to get to the black diamond run," Flaxie said.

"The searchlights and bonfires have been re-established on the hill, Flaxie. Perhaps the brunt of the path missed the ski trails."

Within minutes, the first returning squad of snowmobiles surged into base camp carrying a few who had been able to pull themselves out and flag down the patrol.

"Ah, that is good news," Bodine announced. "The regular patrols hunkered under rock cliffs when the avalanche hit, and they have brought four skiers down with them. No one is harmed beyond frost-bite."

Marceau noticed Flaxie in a fixed gaze. "Did you hear that, Flaxie? The first ones rescued are in good shape."

Wrapping her arms around her uncle, Flaxie moaned, "When this happens I always think of Mama and Papa."

"Of course, my dear, I am remiss not to remember. It was like yesterday . . . so unexpected."

With the comfort of his gentle hug, she sighed her acceptance.

3

Avalanche Rescue

Logan's words were swept up in the roar that was outrunning the skiers. "Marianne! Marianne! Over here! Follow me, don't look back—ski as fast as you can!"

Tumbling and turning, his mind grasped at procedures for survival and preserving air in an avalanche. As the pressure of snow built up over him, a searing pain tore at his right boot. Then nothing but heaviness and darkness.

I can't breathe!

Managing to wiggle some mobility, Logan found one of his ski poles and poked it upward in the hope he could be found before he ran out of oxygen.

"If I'm lucky I'll have fifteen minutes of air, then I start inhaling my carbon dioxide. At least that will put me to sleep and death should be painless."

Somewhere in the distance, he heard sirens and knew he must be upright. Fighting as he could, he lost consciousness until he felt frantic scratching near his face and the muzzle of a Bernese Mountain Dog. In the euphoria of gratitude that he had been snatched from the grasp of death, he was overwhelmed to the brink of tears.

Logan gasped between gulps of air.

"Merci! Merci! I have a friend with me, her name is Marianne . . . please save her."

A kindly voice offered assurance. "Take it easy, pal, we'll get you out first. Many rescuers are here and we are working as hard as we can."

Unable to stand on his own, he was wrapped in a thermal blanket and loaded onto a dogsled for transport to the emergency center.

Through the blazing sun, he squinted at a woman in a blue ski suit being placed behind a snowmobile driver to accompany his descent.

"Marianne, is that you?"

"Oui, Logan, we have survived."

To Logan, the dog sled took forever down the mountain and his worst thoughts surged through his brain. Foremost was the Grand Marceau and concern that his position could be in jeopardy.

Emergency vehicles screamed up the narrow road to the Grand Marceau, followed by journalists and camera-carrying onlookers. Roberto Dion assembled stanchions and barrier lines to keep the hotel from flooding with bystanders.

"Hans," Dion barked, "see that only official members of the rescue group are admitted beyond this point. Recruit from the bellboys to help."

At the same moment, Bodine marched toward his assembly platform in the arrival parking lot. In his uniform and peaked hat, he was easily recognizable over the crowd.

Dion rushed to him. "Any update, Monsieur Bodine?"

Hunter Bodine had been an alpine ranger all his adult years and knew this terrain well. His stern demeanor was not unusual, but his stature sagged with the ultimate test of organization and communication. Despite the disaster's commotion, his eyes went to Flaxie.

"Please convey to Monsieur Marceau that we recovered four more survivors thanks to the Bernese rescue. A chopper is being dispatched to Widow's Peak momentarily to two of the injured. Two more are being brought down by dog sled."

"Oui, Monsieur, that is good news," Dion said with a nod, then turned to seek out the hotel owner.

Bernard Marceau was assisting in the conference room where he could be of service. The dining room's plated service was closed, and a brunch buffet was organized in the ballroom. Extra staff was sent out to join Bodine's search party.

"Monsieur Marceau, they are bringing down four survivors. No word of any victims at this point, so that is good news."

Bernard looked up confused.

"There is no good news here, only hope."

"Monsieur Marceau, it is early yet," Bodine consoled. "The avalanche did not hit the trails too hard as the weight went into the high forest. Calm and patience is the best plan."

Bernard Marceau was equipped to stand in the elements in his sheepskin coat, laced snow boots, and furry flap hat. At his side, Flaxie had a hot chocolate pack strapped to her back supplying warmth to survivors and rescuers.

With the snowmobile in view, a yelping cheer of support rose to signal its success.

Marianne dismounted on her own, and as the dog sled arrived, she instinctively bolted to help Logan. He was trying desperately to stand on an injured ankle but attempting to camouflage his injury.

"Logan, you are hurt. Let them take you to the hospital, it could be broken."

"No, Marianne, I will not give up. Let me have your arm."

Waiting near Bodine, Flaxie moved closer to the rescue. Curious about the injured arrivals, she observed the interaction between the pair and stepped forward.

"Monsieur, my name is Flaxie Marceau. I see you are injured, so let the medics have a look at least. In the meantime what can I do?"

"Flaxie Marceau?"

His face paled not from the pain but by her name alone. Taken off guard, he was speechless how to respond so soon. Marianne did her best to intercede.

"You have hot chocolate—I sure could use a cup. It's generous of you and the hotel to be so hospitable."

Ranger Bodine interrupted with formality and asked the skiers for identification.

"I'm glad you're both alive and well but you must be in shock and freezing. As a precaution, you each need a medical review at the emergency tent before you leave the area, and take that boot off to control swelling. Also, leave contact information so we can follow up."

Bodine raised himself, with a pat on the back for Logan and a handshake to Marianne.

Right away, Flaxie noticed Logan's gaze linger her way, and his awkward effort to conceal his injury.

Who is he? Such a handsome man and with such magnetism.

Bernard Marceau called Flaxie to bring the hot drinks to the next snowmobile. Her head flung back to look at the stranger again before turning to follow her uncle.

A medical assistant rushed to Logan to make a report. The volunteer was a retired militia, a German recruit from Grenoble.

"Your name, Sir?" she asked.

"There's no need for a report, I'm sure I'll be fine," Logan insisted.

She remained firm in her position. "I'm sorry, Sir. It's required before you can leave the area. We'll get that ankle checked and you can rest in the warmth of the hotel before you decide if you can leave under your power."

With Marianne on his right side, he put his weight on the injured ankle, and despite his defiance, he grimaced.

"It's bad, isn't it Logan?"

"If the medics ice and tape it up, I'll be no worse for wear."

The pair hobbled to the first aid zone, where Logan propped his foot on a chair and cushion.

"Let's see, Monsieur, what the damage is."

A young technician released the ski boot clasps and stopped when Logan flinched. "I didn't catch your name, do you have an assessment report from the rescue team?"

"Not yet. My name's Logan."

"Easy . . . I'll release the boot's pressure and pull it away gently, alright?"

Logan clenched his jaw and tightened his white knuckle grip.

"Ah, it's already swelling," the technician said. He moved his figures deftly around the foot and ankle looking for broken bones. "It seems you are lucky today, Logan. I can't feel a fracture, but you need an x-ray to be certain."

Logan leaned forward with his eyes pleading. "Can you

fix me up for today with freezing, taping, or a temporary cast? Please, I must attend an appointment this afternoon."

Marianne employed her wiles. "We would be eternally grateful. This is a once-in-a-lifetime opportunity and we must show up. I beg of you, Monsieur, if there is anything at all you can do so he can walk, it would mean a great deal."

The technician looked down at his medical bag pondering his options.

"Take Tylenol for pain . . . Wait here, I'll see if I can find an air cast. You can wear it under your clothing without anyone noticing it. But you must keep ice on it and raised whenever possible."

Logan eyed the medic's badge. "Oui, Arlo, I will certainly do as you recommend. We are most grateful."

"But complete this assessment report while I tape and set your ankle in the apparatus."

While in first aid, another half a dozen survivors arrived in worse shape, and moments later, Arlo returned.

"There you go, Logan, I must see to the new arrivals. I hope your appointment goes well."

4

Grand Introductions

By early afternoon the rescue operation was tapering back. The conference room had been disbanded, however, the ranger's checkpoint tent still stood near the hotel portico.

Hunter Bodine sought out Bernard Marceau for an update, finding him in his office poring over letters and documents in the great book.

"Monsieur Marceau, most skiers have been accounted for with no fatalities to report. Only three have not reported, but we have a campaign in Chamonix and the villages to look for guests who may have returned without following check-out procedures."

Marceau raised his head with relief.

"Hopefully, they'll be found shortly. It is most unfortunate to have a tragedy, especially at Christmas. I don't mean to dig up old wounds, but this is a painful reminder."

"We still have two dog teams and a crew of snowmobilers on the slopes for another few hours. The first team has moved over to Argentière and the Grands Montet slopes that were hit worse. By tonight, I expect we can vacate the space you have allotted to the rescue."

"Take as long as you need, Hunter. If we can do anything else, tell Monsieur Dion."

Weighted in thought, Bernard rechecked and itemized notes for the apprentice and his travel arrangements.

"Logan Powell is due at the 2 p.m. orientation."

The chef looked at his watch. "Punctuality will be the first test. If he does not present himself precisely, I'll make the cancellation call."

He was anxiously staring at the phone on his desk when Flaxie entered his office.

"Uncle, it's been a harrowing morning to be sure, but the disaster team worked like a charm. There are no serious injuries."

She bit her lip to ask about one of the skiers. "Did you see the couple from Paris early on? The woman was under her power, but the man had a leg injury. I didn't get his name but I'll recheck with Bodine to see who he might be."

"Suit yourself. I don't recall such a couple. Did you catch any more information?"

Flaxie struggled to recall anything. "I believe the fellow called her Marianne."

"Sorry I can't help. Let me know if you have success with the ranger."

Only a few members of the alpine patrol remained at the rescue station when Flaxie arrived.

Hunter Bodine always noticed Flaxie whenever he was at

the hotel, often searching her eyes for a glimmer of reciprocation of his feelings but seeing nothing.

He tipped his hat in a gentlemanly gesture. "Allo, Mademoiselle Marceau, can I be of help."

"You know to call me Flaxie, Hunter. Could I have a look at the injury reports of the skiers brought down from the mountain?"

From a paper stack, he pulled out a summary from the medics' treatments.

"Apart from bruising and a few stitches, we have a broken arm, a suspected rib fracture, knee displacement, and a sprained ankle."

"Who were the ones with the knee displacement and ankle?"

"Why are you so curious?"

"We expect a visitor today who has yet to show."

"The knee displacement was a man in his fifties from Geneva, and the sprained ankle was a young man from Paris. Name is Logan Powell."

"Logan Powell. Do you remember what he looked like?"

"I'm afraid I didn't attend to him. He was sent right away to the medical tent and treated by Arlo but he's been dismissed."

"Thank you, Hunter, I don't expect to need any further information."

It was the Grand Marceau's long-standing tradition to provide pomp and ceremony to welcome a new sous-chef, even for short-term residency. Ingrid coordinated the formality with Roberto Dion, with a receiving line in a column in the hallway outside the main dining room.

"Ingrid, he's not here," Marceau balked. "Perhaps you were premature in preparing a reception."

"He will be here, I know it, Bernard. Put on your chef's jacket and queue up."

Roberto Dion watched the door for anyone he would not recognize as a registered guest, and at ten minutes to two, a well-dressed, handsome couple entered the lobby, the man with an ever-so-slight limp. He rushed to greet the pair.

"Bonjour and welcome to the Grand Marceau, I am the hotel manager. Do you wish a room or for check-in?"

"The name is Logan Powell. I have an appointment with the esteemed Bernard Marceau."

Roberto glanced toward the receiving line with a nod to Ingrid to indicate the sous-chef's presence. From across the hall, she motioned back with barely a sigh.

"Bernard, he is here."

Ingrid had never seen her boss show such relief. He quickly took his place at the head of the queue, with Flaxie squeezing in next.

Maintaining a suitable pace through the lobby to the main dining room was agonizing for Logan. Marianne held his elbow firmly for support and every few steps she slowed on the pretense of chatter.

When he set eyes on the renowned chef standing crisp and white in his distinguished authority, he picked up his pace and the room slowed as he soaked in the procession's elegance and pomp.

Looking beyond the master chef Bernard Marceau's outstretched hand, his eyes fell on the beautiful Flaxie beside him.

Flaxie froze in thought.

It's the man from this morning. I couldn't forget those violet-blue eyes. How is he managing to stand on a sprained ankle?

Logan's stare was transfixed on Flaxie.

I had no idea Chef Marceau had such a beautiful daughter. It came as a surprise this morning.

Ingrid observed the hesitation and jumped in to advance the introductions. She was a vision herself with her golden braids pinned atop her head.

She curtsied graciously in a festive red skirt. "Monsieur Powell, please, I'd like you to meet Chef Bernard Marceau. We are glad that you'll sojourn with us over the holidays. I am Ingrid Straussman, the head housekeeper, and I will assist however I can."

Bernard Marceau watched Logan's every inflection and was taken aback on how similar he was to himself as a young man.

I'm pleased that he has left the Parisian arrogance behind, with no attitude on his shoulder. He seems congenial. It's good to bring some youth into an old establishment . . . perhaps I was quick to prejudge.

"Welcome, Monsieur Powell. Director Morningside sent glowing reports of your expertise at the George. We, at Grand Marceau, pride ourselves on professionalism and the highest quality of food and service and everyone looks forward to your contribution."

"Your words are kind, Chef Marceau. I assure you I will do my best not to disappoint."

Marianne nudged his elbow.

"Ah, if I may introduce my assistant, Marianne. She has studied with me in Paris for several years. When people work together they understand one another and are more proficient."

Ingrid smiled at Logan's analogy. "You are so right, Monsieur Powell, it comes down to anticipating before one knows for themselves, correct?"

Marianne blushed. "You are intuitive, Madame

Straussman. Thank you for including me at the Grand Marceau."

"It's our pleasure, Marianne. If you have no objections, I think we will be fine roommates."

With formalities over, lively greetings were exchanged up and down the line among the reception's cooks, servers, porters, and workers.

Marceau chuckled to himself, "It's like an old-fashioned family reunion. I see that I do not need to worry."

Until the chef began the orientation, Logan forgot about the ankle sprain. He was quickly reminded that he'd need exact step placement to avoid a visible sign of his pain.

"Preparations will begin soon for the evening meal, Monsieur Powell," Bernard said. "Please join me in my office to review my notes as there is much planning for the Christmas festivities."

Flaxie was gratified to watch Logan progress to her uncle's office, knowing that the great, secret book would be revealed to another for the first time in many years.

As the flock of staff dispersed, Roberto dispatched Marianne's luggage to Ingrid's room, and Logan's to a modest suite assigned on the fourth.

In no time, Logan and Marceau marched together into the kitchen in unison except for the younger's slight limp.

The cooking tables were immaculate to meet Marceau's standards, with polished work stations, burnished copper pots hanging on upper racks, and spices measured meticulously at each cooking surface. The prep crew, pristinely attired, waited in position, and Ingrid and Flaxie inspected in silence.

All eyes and ears followed Marceau as he spoke.

"I have taken the liberty of drawing a map with the names

A Wenceslas Christmas

of each assigned member by their service station. However, anyone here will be eager to fill you in as needed."

Marceau gestured to printed notes pinned throughout the kitchen. "Tonight's menu is posted over every cooking area, and as you would anticipate, the ingredients are measured and ready.

"Magnon, Trudel, and Cobb will show you the cold storage and bakeries later. For now, I'll go through our routine and procedures while Juliette, our dessert prep manager, will take Marianne on a tour."

With arms swinging, Marceau marched toward the windowed office in the far corner, satisfied but impatient now that he could focus on the Paris competition.

Logan was awed by the chef's sanctuary, with one wall lined with books and culinary guides and a shelf adorned with awards and framed photos.

A plush leather sofa was in the corner and near the window, with a straight vision to the cooking area, was the two-hundred-year-old desk used by generations of Marceau's ancestors.

"The first day my father allowed me into this office, I was knee-high but I was impacted by the smell of books and ledgers. The pure reverence overwhelmed me. I watched my father pore over the great book, jotting notes hither and yon, then I'd follow him to the kitchen where he would prepare a magnificent meal."

Bernard unlocked a heritage Louis XIV carved bureau and lifted out the strapped leather volume.

"This, my dear friend, represents the lives of Marceaus for the last two hundred years. Every birth in the family is also recorded here, so guard this well." Marceau bellowed at the irony.

"Everything you need to know is here: where to find the best morels and the sweetest new potatoes, the contact at the Italian delicatessen in Fournier, the farmer with the most flavorful herbs on the trail west of Chamonix near Les Praz, the secret blend of cheese for our famous raclette. Best of all, I say, are recipes and sauces for everything that has ever been prepared at the Grand Marceau.

"The menus are prepared one week in advance based on the boucher market's offerings and the wares of the seafood merchant in Cannes. We buy fresh meats and produce from local farmers, and Flaxie could accompany you to assist with choices. Keep in mind that every skier craves raclette, Swiss fondue, and tartiflette, so stock well with cheeses, butter, new potatoes, cornichons, and pickled accompaniments."

Logan was awestruck that he had been elevated to the inner world of Marceau.

"I feel like a child in a toy store at Christmas. This is incredibly wondrous. I assure you, I will guard this with my life."

Marceau leaned back in his leather armchair.

"You know, Logan, I was ambivalent about sharing my kitchen and secrets. The King George hotel has been generous to ensure I attend the Michelin event, but I had misgivings about giving up the reins even for a few weeks. I must say, that my pride and joy above the Michelin star is my niece, Flaxie. Rely on her experience and wisdom and you will succeed here. For business aspects, Monsieur Dion and Madame Straussman will guide you."

"Sir, I appreciate your protectiveness of the Grand Marceau. I will proudly stand in your stead and wish you the greatest of success in Paris."

As Logan's words sealed the deal, Marceau rose out of his chair. "Now that the dining room is in your hands, Logan, I must attend to my packing. I will depart directly after breakfast in the morning. For now, wander about and get a handle on the hotel. We will meet back in the main kitchen at 4 p.m. to commence cooking."

Logan winced as he put his weight on his bad ankle but Marceau did not notice.

5

The Chef Exchange

The kitchen staff were positioning poinsettias and holly in the foyer when Hunter Bodine passed through. He stopped at the reception. News had circulated of Chef Marceau's planned trip to Paris and Hunter thought it would be opportune to be gallant during his absence.

"Is Flaxie available?"

Roberto Dion looked up in surprise. "Monsieur Bodine, I'll be sure to let her know you enquired, however, we have received a new sous-chef and we're amid orientation."

Sensing his words had been abrupt, he softened them. "Your crew did a fine job with the search and rescue today. We are indebted to you and your staff."

"All in a day's work, Monsieur."

Mildly dejected, Bodine patted the desk and nodded. As he neared the exit, he passed Logan and Ingrid touring the foyer. He swung around to them.

A Wenceslas Christmas

"Madame Straussman, I understand the hotel has taken on a new sous-chef during Monsieur Marceau's absence."

In mid-sentence, it occurred to him that this may be the very person. Logan smiled at the awkwardness and offered a handshake.

"Hello, Ranger Bodine, I'm Logan Powell, the sous-chef substitution while the chef is away. I saw you working at the avalanche rescue and I expect I'll see more of you in the future."

"Of course. What do I call you? Monsieur Powell or Chef Powell?" Hunter searched clumsily for a title then changed direction. "Have we met before?"

"When I am working, I'll respond to Chef Powell. However, as I'm on my own time at the present, Logan will do fine."

"Very well then. I'll be off. Perhaps I'll see you around tomorrow."

Bodine felt overwhelmed and disgruntled that the new sous-chef was a charming, handsome man with a pleasant persona, an intrusion on his territory.

Flaxie flounced down the center stairs and steered directly toward Logan and Ingrid. Her hair was pulled back into a ribbon and her long curls cascaded over her shoulders.

With her eyes lingering on Logan, she felt a flirtatious ownership. "There you are. How'd it go with Uncle Bernard?"

Although Ingrid had discussed Flaxie's social isolation in the Alps with Bernard, the opportunity to send her to finishing school was not well received. In recent years, she had dalliances with several potential suitors but tired of them quickly. Ingrid was elated by the magnetism between the two and made her excuses, sensing three's a crowd.

"Your uncle and I had a fine talk," Logan said. "He assured me I could count on you to assist at the boucher markets and to advise me as I need."

"Of course . . . Logan, I have a question on my mind.

"Anything. What is it?"

"When you came down the slope with the dog sled, I introduced myself, but you looked at me as if you'd seen a ghost. I'm curious about what you were thinking."

"Ah, ha, I've been caught red-handed. Marianne and I planned to burn off pre-appointment jitters by skiing. Looking back, that was not a good choice."

He gestured to his right ankle. "I knew I'd wrenched something in the tumble and I thought that my chances here with Chef Marceau might be ruined. I froze at hearing your name, concerned that your uncle could withdraw this opportunity."

"Appearances indicate you've recovered quickly, or so it seems. With a woman's intuition, I see you're suffering, but don't worry. I won't say anything—Uncle Bernard never needs to know."

"I am grateful, Flaxie, if I may call you by that."

"Of course, all my friends and family use it. It's an odd name, but my father decided on it once it was determined my hair was flaxen blond. I'm named after my mother, Francesca, and they were going to nickname me Fanny, but Uncle Bernard objected."

For a nervous moment, neither said anything until Logan gestured to the clock behind reception.

"I need to change to be in the kitchen shortly. Is there an elevator to the fourth floor? I don't want to press my luck with this ankle."

"Follow me. I won't walk fast so you can keep up," Flaxie teased, then led off with an exaggerated skip in her step.

Bernard Marceau strode into the kitchen and interrupted as Logan perused the menus with Marianne. "Ah, ha, Monsieur Powell, you seem ready."

He eyed Logan with a gentle scold. "Right away we'll get you into a Grand Marceau jacket and sous hat, as that King George uniform must go."

"It'll be an honor," Logan said.

"At precisely four o'clock, you ring the dinner gong on this long tapestry cord. The staff will gather around and you will recite the complete menu with details of the preparation and sauces. Then the specialty items and dietary requirements will be addressed."

Flaxie smirked at the astonishment on Logan's face as he hadn't been versed with the menu or sauces.

Marceau froze at Logan's expression, then burst into robust laughter. "Ah, ha, you were thinking I expected you to recite it?"

Chuckles rippled to the staff at Marceau's dry humor, but the portly chef was mostly pleased with himself.

"Instead, for this evening, Chef Powell, I am asking Monsieur Magnon to describe the appetizers, Monsieur Trudel the main entrées, Monsieur Cobb the specials, and Madame Juliette will list the delectable desserts.

"Our head sommelier will itemize the wines and aperitifs, then Flaxie will provide a tasting of dessert cheeses. Of course, I will be standing right here, should anyone have questions. Pretend that I am a speaking statue."

Bernard found he enjoyed the levity of his humor at Logan's expense. "Well then, we shall begin."

Then to Marceau's amusement, Logan pulled the tapestry cord. Instantly a troupe of prep staff brought out sampling platters, each to be described in detail. Logan was familiar with this process from the Paris hotels.

Following the pre-meal custom, the staff queued in a pre-arranged order to sample the smorgasbord of delicacies.

At precisely 4:30 p.m. Chef Marceau requested Logan to accompany him to the maître d' podium to review the reservation lists and for a walk-about inspection of the dining room.

"Is this different from the King George?" Bernard enquired.

"The ambiance is much better here at the Grand, more subdued, and the samplings were exceedingly impressive. It would make a great study to find any fault."

"I appreciate your candor, Chef Powell, but if you can lend me any advice for my participation at the international gourmet event, I'd take it wisely."

"Why, Sir, your reputation precedes you, I would not make any adjustments."

Logan rallied on his diplomacy to placate his esteemed peer. "I were to comment, I would tell you that Director Morningside's favorite dish is a good tartiflette with Savoyard cheese or the lamb tagliatelle with lemon, olive, and chermoula sauce."

The two chefs enjoyed a burst of laughter that continued as Marceau embraced the irony.

"And in return . . . I should say that Monsieur Dion favors the raclette or mashed potato and minced Parmentier, but of course, the precise palate would choose our Torte Lorraine from Provence."

Bernard raised his finger. "But Logan, you omit the unique tastes of the King George's resident chef, Augustus, I believe?"

"Ah, you have caught me on being deliberate. Perhaps

A Wenceslas Christmas

that is something you can find out for yourself—but conceal your recipe if you wish it to be your signature dish."

Marceau looked for a long moment into Logan's eyes. "Another time, I would like to hear that story."

The evening meal progressed splendidly with many compliments sent back to the kitchen. In fact, Bernard Marceau found himself idle and retreated to his quarters early to resume his packing. He encountered Ingrid as he neared the elevator.

"Ingrid, it has been a long day. Please give my apologies, but I will retire early to finish collecting the necessary travel outfits and personals. I'll see you in the morning before I leave."

With a sigh and a heave, he paused to look into her worried, blue eyes.

"I see that you are worn out, Bernard, as a great deal has happened today. Paris is the city of lights and is marvelous. Take time to see the sights and not settle entirely in the menus. Perhaps one day you and I could take a nice spring visit."

Ingrid tilted her head to toy with him for a response, but his mind was already elsewhere.

"Goodnight, Ingrid. I'd like a last cup of your espresso in the morning. We'll have time to watch the sun come up over Mont Blanc."

Deep inside, he was urged to take her in his arms and hold her, but instead, he turned away.

Most of the staff had gone to their homes in the village or to staff quarters, with some to discos and night cafés.

Flaxie and Marianne loitered in the kitchen with glasses of wine, talking about the hotel, Paris, old boyfriends, and a bit of staff gossip.

"It's nice to have you here, Marianne—I'm enjoying the girl talk."

Logan was engrossed in the great leather book in Marceau's office when Marianne called goodnight from the hall. As he began to bundle the pages, a yellowed envelope slipped to the floor from the back of the volume. He noticed it was from a law firm in Paris. Written across the face of the envelope were the words, 'her 25th birthday'.

He heard Flaxie approaching and quickly shoved the envelope back into place and strapped the bindings together.

"Chef Powell, I've been to the freezer and I brought an ice pack. I insist you put your ankle up."

She pulled out a footstool from under the bureau and perched it beside the swivel chair. Logan's face showed his surprise and a tinge of delight too.

"My instinct is to refuse, but I admit that's a good idea."

He eased his right foot onto the cushioned bench. Delicately, she untied his shoelace and edged his cuff above the air cast. He was struck by the intimacy of her touch.

"Logan, your ankle is purple! Don't you move. I'll get more ice."

She put her finger to her lips to prevent his objection and closed the office door lest anyone else observe his condition. When she returned with more ice, his face was ashen with pain, his jaw taut, and his eyes were pinched tight.

"You can have a Tylenol for the pain, or shall I get you a good stiff whiskey? Your choice."

"The whiskey, please!"

Looking up like a puppy without a home, Logan stumbled over his words. "I didn't plan this to get your attention."

He laughed at his predicament. "I don't deserve your discretion but I'm very grateful."

Their chats ranged from a whiskey salute to Chef Marceau to toasts about stories in life, then wound down to concede that the next obstacle was to move Logan in this condition.

"Somehow we'll get you up to your room. In the morning I'll get First Aid to fix you up. After Uncle Bernard has departed, the hotel doctor can take a look at this."

Getting Logan's shoe back on was hopeless and his inebriation made him a deadweight.

"I have an idea, Logan, but you must wait here."

Ernesto, one of the night doormen, was pacing on the outer veranda, rubbing his hands to keep warm. Explaining the dilemma, Flaxie put on his heavy winter hotel coat and continued pacing on his behalf.

Half an hour later, Ernesto returned with an amused grin. "He's out cold on his bed."

Flaxie tried to tip him for his silence and he refused but relented with a quick kiss on his cheek.

"Anytime, Flaxie!"

6

Departure to Paris

At 6 a.m., Bernard was completing the grooming of his distinguished, white beard when he remembered his espresso with Ingrid. He readied himself quickly and hurried, not to keep her waiting.

At the panorama sunroom, Ingrid ambled through the arch with a tray, in a festive alpine apron.

"Your timing is perfect, Bernard."

"I have never missed an appointment in my life," he announced.

"I'd like to think I'm more than an appointment on your calendar, Bernard."

"Well, of course, Ingrid, you are the light of my life and the master of my domain."

"You're terrible at compliments, Bernard," Ingrid teased him with a wry smile. "Perhaps when you return from Paris, you'll see me a bit differently . . . you know it's the little things that are important."

She offered him a steaming cup, then snuggled on the sofa beside him, pulling her legs underneath her skirt.

"Are the Paris folk sending a limousine for you? I looked up the travel routing and it is complicated from Chamonix. Although the Mont Blanc express train would be more scenic, you'd have to change along the way before arriving in Paris."

"Morningside insisted on sending their chauffeur to ensure a comfortable journey. The car should arrive by nine but I won't get to Paris until the early afternoon. There's plenty to contemplate on the way and perhaps I'll read a good mystery."

"It's good to see you have given up on your worries about the new sous-chef. Logan seems to be a fine man and competent. Perhaps you'll get a bonus with your protégé . . . I'm sure sparks flew between him and Flaxie."

At first, Bernard was slow to comprehend. "Sparks! You mean romance?"

"Of course, it's romantic. Flaxie is a beautiful young woman with no shortage of suitors, but not many have been this interesting."

"I assumed that Hunter Bodine would get around to courting her. Perhaps it's too late for him."

"Well, it's not up to us who her heart decides to follow. I believe in fate, that each person is meant to find their soulmate in life. But don't set your concerns on Flaxie, Bernard, as you'll only be away for three weeks."

"I was up late arranging menu suggestions and I prepared my case of special herbs that I got a few days ago at Les Praz. Then I packed my preferred oils from the Italian shop in Chamonix, and of course, my unique cheeses that won't be available in Paris. My valise will not leave me."

"Can I do anything to help you, Bernard? I'll miss you and my wishes will travel to Paris too, that you will be suitably rewarded in the competition for your creativity and excellence.

"It's our first Christmas apart in all the years I've been here. I have a small present for you but if you don't mind I'll wait until you come home to give it to you."

Ingrid blushed, expecting that the sentiment wouldn't have occurred to Bernard.

"Oh my goodness, Christmas presents! I hadn't gotten around to that," he said. "Something must be left under the tree for Flaxie." Frantically his eyes pleaded. "Please, Ingrid . . . jewelry, perfume, or something suitable."

"Don't worry, Bernard. I was thinking of an item from the family suite . . . maybe meaningful and sentimental from her mother. If you don't object, it's time for a visit."

"Yes, of course, you know best. The keys are in my desk."

Taking a step back, he sighed with relief but held inside his sadness that he had delegated that responsibility of Christmas.

Flaxie's arrival brightened his morning, knowing her uncle's preferred spot for the first espresso of the day.

"Allo, Uncle Bernard. I thought I'd find the two of you here."

"Yes, I'm enjoying the peace before I go to the city where no one sleeps at night."

"The ranger has posted the red flag for the morning. Although the avalanche level was low, they found a man on Les Grands Montet slopes last night who had succumbed. The ranger's unit will shoot down a few ice cliffs from the peak, and we'll hear the cannons booming. It's a somber feeling that a vibrant being with the zest of life is no longer among the living."

"Oh, Mon Dieu!" Ingrid gasped. "I hadn't heard about the fatality. Has everyone else been accounted for?"

"Apparently."

"Hunter Bodine must have been here very early to have informed you," Marceau said, speculating that the ranger's presence might have reflected on his niece.

Flaxie blushed. "I've known Hunter for years, but we've always only been friends. I'd like it to remain that way. Will you be coming to the dining room for breakfast, Uncle Bernard?"

"Non, it is Monsieur Powell's forum for now, but give him an embossed Grand Marceau uniform as he was wearing one from Paris." He winked at her. "Otherwise, of course, I'd appreciate a basket of delicacies for my car journey to Paris."

"It's alright, Flaxie," Ingrid said. "I would be delighted to prepare the basket for your uncle." With determination she rose to depart, knowing his favorites.

Early rising guests were beginning to saunter into the main dining when Flaxie bounded past the host.

"Bonjour, excusez-moi!"

She halted to peer through the revolving door's window to catch a glimpse of Logan. Rising to her tiptoes, it occurred to her that she felt a flutter to see him.

Logan turned as she came toward him. "Bonjour, Flaxie. I kept the ice on as long as possible and there seems to be some improvement in the swelling. Marianne helped to wrap it and set the air cast. Thank you for your kindness to me."

Why would he call Marianne? I'm the one that nursed him to the early hours.

"I'm not familiar with your schedule, Flaxie, but I would

like to confer with you after breakfast if you have time."

Flaxie was confused by his sudden formality. "Absolutely. I thought I'd check with you first to see if I could help. I have morning rounds with department managers to review reservations and hotel events. We have yet to finalize the New Year's Eve gala plans so I can book the printers."

Logan was surprised that the annual event's details were not yet concluded. "Of course, the gala must be the pinnacle event of Mont Blanc and I'll commit to that."

Passing through the lobby, Flaxie stopped beside Ingrid to watch Ernesto loading her uncle's trunks into a black limo in the portico. It seemed to her that Marceau, in his sixties, appeared nervous about leaving home this trip.

"My poor Uncle Bernard, I wish I could go with him," she said. Ingrid was quiet, and Flaxie observed concern and worry on her face.

My goodness, they are a pair, each belongs with the other. Ingrid raised me with the love of my mother and she stood faithfully by him through thick and thin. She is being torn apart by his departure and he doesn't even look at her.

Flaxie put her arm lovingly around Ingrid.

"Thank you for encouraging Uncle to go. I know he wouldn't have come to such a decision without you. Someday soon he will realize that his guardian angel is standing right here beside him."

"You are too kind, Flaxie, but the heart always does what it wants. Time will tell."

With his luggage stowed, Marceau returned to the lobby for a proper farewell. Roberto Dion stood at attention expecting final instructions from his boss.

"Monsieur Dion, I have full confidence that you'll do a

fine job. Let's hope there won't be another avalanche in these weeks. If yesterday was a test, you excelled."

Marceau exchanged a hearty handshake with his manager then remembered the packet in his jacket.

"Please distribute these to your staff on Christmas Eve. And Merry Christmas, my friend."

He turned to the ladies. "Flaxie take care of the hotel . . . and your heart too while I am gone. I will send a prayer for you every night as I always have."

A long embrace followed that flowed with emotion in the tradition of the Marceaus.

Ingrid had taken a step back, unsure of what to expect from this man she admired so much. Yet she knew he had learned to take her for granted.

"Dear Ingrid, I'll remember that you promised me a dance at the gala when I return."

Holding her at arms-length, he looked slowly, seeing her differently this time. Leaning closer, he put a hand gently on her chin, and his kiss on the cheek aroused a surprising feeling. She closed her eyes and lingered in his embrace with the last remembrance of his cologne and a soft brush of his whiskers.

As his coattails vanished through the revolving doors and the limo coasted into the morning darkness, Logan Powell rushed into the lobby. "I'm too late. I wanted to thank Chef Marceau and wish him well."

"Don't worry, he knows," Flaxie said. "Sometimes goodbyes get to be a bit much. If he wished any last words or warning, he would have sought you out himself."

"I suppose you know him best, but I still feel like I missed out."

The three were about to disperse when Hunter Bodine

entered the revolving door. His eyes went to Flaxie with an intended smile but faded as Logan was standing close to her.

"Bonjour, Ladies, and Gentleman. We are disbanding the relay point, and I'll be returning to the ranger station above Chamonix."

He bit his tongue, looking at Ingrid, then Logan, waiting until it was apparent he sought a moment of privacy with Flaxie.

"Oh, excuse me, Ranger Bodine, I must be about my chores," Ingrid said with a curtsy.

Logan's voice became stern as he noticed Bodine placing his hand on Flaxie's elbow to steer her away for a private conversation. "Of course, Monsieur Bodine, I'll talk with Mademoiselle Marceau later."

Instead of retreating to the kitchens, Logan ambled over to Roberto Dion who was also on watch.

"It seems that Miss Marceau has an admirer," he said, prying for an assessment from the manager.

"He's what you call a ladies' man. Been in the area for several years and enjoyed courting many local ladies as well as visitors. He and Flaxie are good friends, but if he'd been keenly interested, he's had many an opportunity.

Roberto leaned closer to Logan with his voice lowered, accepting the invitation to be an accomplice. "If you want my opinion, he has noticed that he has competition. I've seen the look in Flaxie's eyes when she looks at you." He leaned on his elbow and winked at Logan.

"I'm not sure that I understand what you mean by competition."

"Think about it, Logan. You'll figure it out."

Dion enjoyed a snigger, and Logan remained at the observation post, both pretending not to watch Hunter and Flaxie. As the manager observed every cue, he reported back

A Wenceslas Christmas 51

like he was sharing a secret with an old friend.

"He's nervous, I say he's getting up the nerve to ask her to the New Year's Eve gala. He should have had the gumption to talk to Marceau before he left. She looks surprised and I'm not sure she is giving him a reply. No . . . she's putting him off . . . that she'd have to check her work schedule."

They both watched as Bodine turned to leave with his shoulders down.

"Definitely rejected, I'd say," Dion whispered.

Flaxie spun around and charged directly at Logan and Dion, her face showing a fury Logan had not yet seen.

"I know that the pair of you were watching. How dare you? I demand respect for my privacy. Furthermore, I'll have you know that I will go to the ball with whoever I choose. Monsieur Powell, I'd like a word with you in your office."

Dion blushed from the admonishment then apologized before turning his attention to the reception area to ease his humiliation.

Slamming the door, Flaxie stomped straight to the sofa in the office and glared at Logan.

He was calm and direct and spoke first.

"Mademoiselle Marceau, I'm doing my best to fit in here under the brief circumstances. I have worked hard to qualify for this position and I've been tested and rated by my superiors along the way. Do not consider me a novice in need of training."

Flaxie sat up ready to speak.

"No, Flaxie, I'm not finished. It is my right and expectation to become familiar with the staff that includes Roberto Dion, the hotel manager. If it so happens that someone comes into the hotel to speak with you, am I to suddenly become blind and deaf? Yes, you are the niece of the great Bernard Marceau, but that does not give you the authority to berate me in front of other staff. If you have issues with me, be kind enough to address me in private.

"I trust we can put this little tiff behind us and continue with a sociable relationship. I look forward to learning from your wisdom and experience. Shall we call a truce?"

During Logan's tirade, Flaxie found the need to humble herself. She was captivated by his eyes and the manner he took charge. The assertive pulse at his temple and the tenseness of his jaw became very appealing.

"My apologies, Chef Powell, I was out of line and behaved badly. Uncle Bernard would be ashamed of me. I would very much like to continue an amicable rapport with you. I'll give my regrets to Monsieur Dion as well."

"That is good. Now, you suggested earlier that we meet to discuss the gala, is this a good time?"

"If we could rendezvous in the café in an hour, I'll gather my notes and last year's promotions. A general outline has already been established, but the specifics of the event need your input."

"Very well, the café in an hour."

7

Logan's Foothold

With an hour to spare before meeting with Flaxie, Logan did a cursory inventory of the cold storage, comparing stock to the week's menus. Chef Marceau had itemized ingredients and recipes until the 16th leaving two more weeks of planning in Logan's hands.

I'll need to go to markets at Les Praz, Argentière, Le Tour, and Chamonix, and Monsieur Trudel's herb garden. Magnon will take a delivery wagon to town for supplies. Flaxie will know the route and markets.

In the privacy of his work, he whispered out loud to himself, "Flaxie, you will be an unexpected challenge. I've never encountered such a distraction to my work before."

Marianne popped her head around the door. "What was that about Flaxie?"

"Ah, Marianne, it's been so busy we haven't had time for a cup of coffee. How is it for you, sharing with Ingrid?"

"It's awesome. She is beautiful . . . exactly like my grandmother but smarter. I love her slight Austrian accent. She has been more than kind to me."

"I'm glad it's going alright."

"I've wondered about the ankle. I've noticed your limp despite your brave face."

"After the lunch break, I'll find the hotel doctor. First Aid is behind the baggage hold."

"Logan, I've been trying to reach Jean-Paul, but he is not answering in Montparnasse. His schedule seldom varies, so I don't know how I keep missing him."

"Jean-Paul adores you of course. Sometimes people make themselves busy when they are lonely. I'm guilty of that as well."

"A lot of that is going on here at the Grand Marceau. Dear Ingrid is another example. Would you believe she's been carrying a torch for Bernard for twenty years? She told me how she arrived at the hotel. With no family or friends in France, she marched herself up the hill and demanded to see old Marceau.

"I envision her like Maria from Sound of Music, standing there at the door with her satchel. They had no opening available so she booked her bag into storage and went about dusting and vacuuming until they made a position for her. I call that hutzpah."

Logan realized Marianne had more on her mind but he looked at the time. The spare hour had dissipated.

"Why don't we have a drink together after the night shift? Like old times," he said.

"Certainly. I should be in the kitchen ricing potatoes for tonight's tartiflette."

Retreating to the culinary prep room, Marianne mumbled her deeper thoughts to herself.

Logan arrived minutes late at the café on the glass-covered veranda. Weaving between the crowded tables, he found Flaxie at a setting by the fireplace with two steaming mugs and a plate of pastries.

"Sorry, I'm late. I have a dilemma and you might have an answer. People and details keep changing my schedule and intentions. Did your uncle find that too?"

"You need to establish boundaries, but also allow a time slot for people who need to talk so they'll feel welcome. Ingrid always watched out for Uncle Bernard as his shadow and bodyguard. If you'd like, I'll have a chat with her. She's feeling lost without him and will rally to know her services are in need."

"Thank you, and yes, please have the chat."

Flaxie opened a file of the entertainment and dining specs from the previous holiday.

"First I'll digress from the gala to discuss Christmas at the hotel. We are fully booked with many families. Uncle asked me to organize the Christmas Eve show in the ballroom.

"We typically host family entertainment before Father Christmas arrives to give out gifts and candy . . . Ingrid takes care of those arrangements. As you can imagine, Uncle Bernard was the ideal Santa so we'll need a replacement. If you don't object, I'm considering asking Monsieur Dion."

"Is the program already in place?"

"Mostly. We have a wonderful play that rollicks with good family fun and laughter. I've hired jesters from the village and have a lead on marionettes in Argentière. A group of bell ringers and Swiss yodelers come every year with a training session that brings out all the children, and the local dance studio sends tap performers."

"Dining is a smorgasbord, I assume?"

"Oh yes, the traditional buffet. Our ethnic feature is raclette and cheese fondue, and of course, everyone uses the chocolate fountain."

She sipped her cappuccino and dabbed a croissant with jam.

Logan pointed at her papers. "There's much more as I can see your file is full."

"For the Boxing Day brunch, you can repeat the menu and schedule from last year."

Logan folded the menus and notes in his valise.

"I have things to say, Flaxie, before you get to the gala. We are only two people, but the workload you describe takes a committee. Let's reschedule the gala planning and include Ingrid and Marianne and anyone else whose participation is appropriate. Your uncle will be proud."

"That's a brilliant idea, Logan . . . er, Chef Powell."

"Also, I need to book a shopping excursion with you to the boucher markets."

"Of course. Usually, the best produce is on Saturday mornings. Does that suit you?"

"First thing Saturday then . . . thank you, Flaxie. This was productive."

As he rose to leave, she said, "We're not finished yet."

"I am sorry but I'm overloaded at the moment, Flaxie. You have my trust to make decisions and you needn't consult with me on everyday things. And thank you for arranging Ingrid's help. That will be a blessing to help me stay on task."

Dumbfounded, she watched Logan cross to the foyer. The limp was improving and his confidant posture told her he had taken charge.

When I was a little girl, Mother told me that it's a big world and that in the Grand, I was living like a princess in a magnificent castle.

She said when the day would come I'd want to seek love, I would need to leave and explore the world.

At 17, Uncle sent me to London for two years of schooling. I made many friends including the handsome Jerrod. I thought he might be the one but I waited for sparks and tingly toes that never came. Today, here I sit at the Grand, and darn it if that man doesn't make my heart flutter and my toes tingle.

Her cappuccino was cold and she rose to take in the ambiance, mixing with families and guests circulating through the lobby.

Strolling along the concourse, she passed quaint shops with garlands and bows and the décor of an Olde English Dickens Christmas, with wooden toys and stuffed teddies, an art gallery, and a chocolaterie.

The Grand Marceau's annual tradition drew crowds to its magnificent twelve-foot fir in the center hall, decked in crimson red and gold baubles, ribbons, tinseled garlands, and twinkling lights. Every child that passed the tree looked up at the magic as she once had.

"Ah, this is indeed the Christmas I know. Logan is right, we must make this year the best to make Uncle Bernard proud."

Encountering Ingrid at the main staircase, Flaxie lit up, pent on her new mission.

"Morning, Ingrid. I was on my way to find you."

"It's like I'm missing my right arm. I'm so used to urging and cajoling your uncle, I'm not sure what to do without him." She straightened her demeanor to hide her unexpected tears.

"Has he called from Paris?"

"Indeed, a brief conversation last night to send his extra

shoes. Hunter will ensure they are shipped from Chamonix."

"And the competition . . . is he satisfied with it?

"Oh, so much! In another zone, in his element. I'm glad he accepted this honor and opportunity as the break has been overdue for him. Paris is a magical world at Christmas especially, with laser light shows, theater, bon marches, and so much life. I envy him."

"He'll be back before you know it. In the meantime, we forgot to foresee that Logan needs an Ingrid too, for those things you do for Uncle. I have too much on my plate to take him on, so I was thinking . . ."

Flaxie paused, watching quizzically, and before her, Ingrid transformed into a mother hen ready to brood.

"Yes, Flaxie I can do that!" Ingrid's girlish charm returned with her broad smile.

"I expect he's in his office or the kitchen."

Whistling, Ingrid flounced away toward the dining room with a twirl of her festive red skirt and pinned, twisted braids.

Logan was thumbing through schedules from last Christmas when Ingrid announced herself ready to be of service.

"You are a lifesaver, Ingrid. I guess Chef Marceau didn't want to share you or he would have had the foresight to loan you to me. Please know you are free to instruct me and make suggestions as you would on any normal day. You have been an obvious complement to Chef Bernard and I hope you will do your best with me as well."

Logan nodded at the great book. "I'm in chef heaven but I confess I'm overwhelmed beyond belief."

"Don't be hard on yourself. Bernard was raised here and trained by his father for over fifty years. You can't expect to equate the great Marceau overnight."

"I could never attain that," he said with a grin. "But I'm glad you understand my view."

"Furthermore, Logan, you must appreciate that each category of service has a crew of sub-staff. For instance, the Grand provides nightly horse and carriage rides, with bonfires and hot chocolate for the guests who come to enjoy our hotel. It's arranged by the concierge and runs like clockwork."

"So you're telling me I don't need to oversee the whole street festival in Chamonix," he teased.

Ingrid was back to her old self, making jokes. "Exactly! That's my job."

Her voice suddenly sobered. "Are you holding something back? Is it to do with Flaxie?"

"You are intuitive, Ingrid. We experienced a brief challenge in hierarchy this morning."

"Monsieur Dion already confided in me. After your talk, she came and apologized to him. I'm impressed by the way you took charge, and Dion had respect for your manner. She can be a runaway filly at times if her leash doesn't get shortened."

"I value her already and I need her confidence and support. She is a remarkable woman, but it's a pleasant complication I've never had to deal with before."

Ingrid looked at him knowingly. "Perhaps you've put your heart on alert, Logan."

Stunned by her revelation, he pondered his feelings.

"I must put my complete focus on my job here. I have dreamed of this career opportunity, but never expected this to unfold."

"But you must let life unfold."

"If I may say with discretion, in the back of my head I'd like to make my mark with Chef Marceau that he might consider taking me on as an apprentice. Perhaps another Michelin star is in the works."

"That sounds admirable and not unrealistic, Logan, but don't get the cart before the horse."

8

Retrospect of a Tragedy

As a precaution, the red avalanche warning flag stayed up at Mont Blanc through the afternoon resulting in an unexpected throng of curious tourists seeking food and entertainment at the Grand.

From the earliest daylight hours, the snow-showing, dog sledding, and cross-country trails had been open to the public.

At the concierge desk, lineups queued through the afternoon for organized horse and carriage departures to the village festival or shuttles to the Vallée Blanche cable car for the panoramic view over Mont Blanc and the glaciers.

Late into the evening, the steady stream of pedestrian traffic continued into the lobby and night bars.

Flaxie crossed paths with Logan only once in the rest of the day as the dining room was overbooked for each meal. Offering her services for bussing under Monsieur Collins, she stopped only when the final evening seating began to thin.

At last, she gave up her apron and went in search of him. Unfortunately, he had departed with Marianne for the promised after-work drink.

Miffed, Flaxie decided to enjoy the outdoor festivities on her own. Even Roberto Dion had left for the day and she was unable to commiserate. At the door, she recognized Ernesto in his greatcoat dutifully greeting guests and holding doors.

"Ernesto, if I wanted to enjoy a pleasant evening on my own without leaving the Marceau, what would I do?"

"Mademoiselle, if I were not on shift, I would take you myself to the disco or for a nice walk under tonight's magnificent snowflakes, to sip our famous hot mulled wine down by the skating rinks."

"Hot mulled wine in the night air! That sounds perfect to me. Thank you, Ernesto, and it was sweet of you to be gallant."

Walking down the slope to the skating rink, Flaxie became aware of Ernesto's large, wonderful snowflakes. On the snowbanks beside the walkway, children were giggling and singing, as they built snowmen and created angels in the snow.

If I could be a child again, everything would be alright.

No sooner had the thought entered her head when she saw Logan and Marianne ahead huddling at the fire pit with brandy glasses, chatting, and laughing like old friends.

In an awkward pause, she considered a retreat when she heard her name.

"Bonsoir, Flaxie. Ernesto said you came this way. May I join you for your walk? It's a beautiful evening."

A Wenceslas Christmas

She knew the voice was Hunter Bodine's, but he was not in his ranger uniform. Wearing a knitted woolen cap, a hooded parka, and ski pants, he looked different and she wondered why she had been so quick to discount him. Instead of the stern ranger façade, tonight he was jovial and relaxed.

"Did you coincidentally happen up this way, or were you looking for me?" Flaxie asked with annoyance.

"I was at the hotel to see Ingrid. She had a package for me to post. How could I come all this way and not seek out the most beautiful girl in all of Mont Blanc."

Laughing, she said, "You're too excessive with the charm, Hunter. What have I done to earn your attention these days? You've been an alpine ranger in these parts for years and you paid me only a few glances."

"My attitude has changed. I've decided I don't want to be a player anymore. I've been thinking of settling down in one of the nearby villages."

"You're putting it rather bluntly, Hunter. You've taken me off guard. Surely you don't mean to infer that I am on your list of candidates."

His eyes twinkled as he smirked. "I'm trying very hard, Flaxie."

"I'm sorry, Hunter, but I must get back to the hotel."

As she turned to leave, he grabbed her arm. "Please Flaxie, let me take you to the New Year's Eve gala. I've been waiting for the right chance to ask you, but you don't give me any encouragement."

Flaxie pulled away dramatically. "Nobody grabs my arm without my permission."

She quickened her step toward the hotel entrance.

The kafuffle drew Logan and Marianne's attention.

Flaxie's distress didn't need an explanation, and Logan was on his feet in an instant to confront the man.

"What's going on here? Flaxie are you alright?"

Logan held firm to Hunter's shoulder. "Oh, it's you, Ranger Bodine. I didn't know you in the dark."

"Everything is fine. I was only extending an invitation to Mademoiselle Marceau and she misunderstood."

In Flaxie's eyes, Logan saw humiliation but something else as their eyes connected—pained regret and longing.

"Come, Flaxie," Marianne said. "We'll adjourn to the hotel for a nightcap. It's chilly out here."

With a welcome arm over Flaxie's shoulder, she steered her from the scene and back up the slope.

Hunter Bodine blended into the crowd and Logan lost sight of him. Resigning to see Flaxie home safely, he jogged to catch up.

Flaxie kept her eyes down. "Thank you both for coming to my rescue but there's no need for concern. If you'll excuse me, I'm rather tired."

Logan watched her start up the staircase without her usual enthusiasm and bounce.

"What should I do, Marianne?"

"Are you worried about what she might be feeling or what you are feeling? When you sort that out, you'll know the answer."

He spun around in annoyance. "And this comes from a wise old spinster? I was wanting a better answer."

"Don't call me a spinster. Indeed I am wise and I thank you, but I also have experience of the heart. Just because Jean-Paul hasn't returned my calls doesn't give you a reason to label me. You brim with passion, Logan, but you have so much to learn about women and love."

"Passion is an essential ingredient for a chef to excel with imaginative, magnificent recipes. You infer that I've caught a virus of sorts."

"Yes, Chef Powell, you are correct. Passion, love and good accompany each other."

"You are an almighty tease, Marianne, and I don't know if I'll forgive you for this."

He melted from her wistful smile and their laugh broke the tension.

"Since Ingrid isn't here to coach you, I'd suggest a midnight phone call to be sure she is alright."

Logan kissed her cheek and bade goodnight.

Flaxie pounced on her bed and sobbed, pressing a framed photo from her dresser close to her heart. Slipping an Elvis CD into the player, she listened sorrowfully to his rendition of 'Blue Christmas'.

Mumbling through tears, she hummed and sang along to the tune.

. . . And when those blue snowflakes start falling
That's when those blue memories start calling
You'll be doing alright, with your Christmas of white
But I'll have a blue, blue, blue Christmas.

"Oh, Mama and Papa, I wished you hadn't left me, especially at Christmastime. My heart only aches for you. Uncle Bernard has gone in search of his dream, and now I find my own heart is aching for another. I need you so, to tell me what to do."

From her closet shelf, she pulled down an old garment box. In a scrapbook packed with photos, news articles, certificates, letters, and keepsakes, she found the tattered newspaper item of the Grenoble tragedy with events of the fateful slide.

> *Witnesses described a thunderous roar of the avalanche. A group of elite skiers, coming off a route near the glaciers, tried to outrun the crush and skied out of bounds unaware they were headed for a precipice. An overhang of ice and snow teetered, then released itself, plunging directly over the escaping skiers.*
>
> *The bodies of Frederick and Francesca Marceau were recovered in the following days. It appears from their catastrophic injuries that their deaths were instantaneous. Family and friends rallied for a vigil at the site near Grenoble.*
>
> *Their only child, eight-year-old Francine Marceau, was with relatives at her family home. Funeral arrangements will be posted in the next days.*

In the years that followed, Flaxie reread every detail a hundred times, wondering what life might have been like if her parents had been spared. Uncle Bernard and Ingrid had more than compensated her with love and she never wanted anything, but now Logan had opened up a feeling of void.

Her recollections of the fateful night were vivid. At the hearth, the family stockings were still hung. In her memory, the suite was festooned with garland, wreaths, sparkling candelabras, and a magnificent blue spruce tree that she had decorated the night before with her family.

Flaxie was eight years at the time and in the care of Ingrid when her parents died. It was dark but not yet supper time and she was punching cut-outs of Ken and Barbie paper dolls, spread prone on the floor. Her family's apartment was on the penthouse floor with two other residences, one for her grandparents, and a smaller one for Uncle Bernard.

She heard rushing feet and gasping in the outer hall, then silence before wailing. Flaxie froze in fear hearing every word and movement.

A Wenceslas Christmas

Where are Mama and Papa, and why are they not here? What has happened?

It wasn't often that the family spoke excitedly in French or German, but on that night prattle varied from high pitches to whispers. When Grandmother and Uncle Bernard opened the door, Flaxie assessed the doom and grief on their faces.

Her room had twin beds with floral chenille spreads and excessive pillows. She buried her head in those cushions and sobbed throughout the night, and beside her, Ingrid stroked her hair and whispered caring reassurances.

Without notice, she was removed from the family residence in the morning and relocated to a smaller suite on the third floor. Ingrid moved into the guest room.

Thereafter, when she visited Uncle Bernard or her grandparents on the upper floor, her eyes always went to her family's door that was locked with a chain.

I need to go there. I want to remember my parents. That is where Christmas ceased. Perhaps I could find something there that is joyous.

Stretching his sprained ankle up on a pillow, Logan plopped onto his bed with hands braced behind his neck, staring at the ceiling. Flaxie's expression stuck in his mind.

"I have to do the right thing here as her uncle has left me in his place. It is more than supervising the kitchen and dining rooms. I can't watch Flaxie suffer."

He reached for the phone on his bedside table and rang through to the third floor.

"Flaxie! I hope I didn't wake you. It's Logan, I wanted to be sure that you are okay . . . you know, from earlier."

"Yes . . . thanks, Logan, I'm fine. I do appreciate your thoughtfulness in checking on me."

"Flaxie, have you been crying?"

"Certainly not, I'm tired. It's been a long day. I'll see you in the morning before breakfast seating. Goodnight, Logan."

"With so much going on in a hotel like this, it's impossible to get a good night's sleep," he bemoaned.

Making notes and researching his competition in the surrounding villages, Logan stayed up into the early morning hours before giving in to slumber.

9

The Boucher Markets

Refreshed by 5 a.m., Logan swept into the kitchen with barely a limp. Marianne and Flaxie had not arrived, and Ingrid waited at the door.

"Good morning, Ingrid, I see you have something on your mind."

"We'll get to that later, Logan. For now, I'd like to remind you that we have a large luncheon party. The Newmans come every year from Windsor and request special treatment from Chef Marceau. They're a bit put out that he's not here, but I assured them you're an excellent substitute. There are twelve in the party.

"I'll make a point to speak to them. Anything else I should know before I begin t0he breakfast menu?"

Ingrid handed him a hand-written note on yellow paper. "I have made a brief list, Chef Powell."

With a quick read, he tucked it in his breast pocket.

"One more thing, Logan. The delivery truck is in for repairs but will be back here for your shopping excursion on Saturday. Otherwise, if you need to get about, Monsieur Dion has a vintage, navy Peugeot in the back lot that you are free to use. It is rusty but reliable."

Behind him, Flaxie bounced into the kitchen, singing and looking like her old self.

"Good morning, Ingrid, and Chef Powell. Did I miss the recitation?" she teased.

"Very funny! You know there's no breakfast monologue, only the standard menu with substitutions. However, I spiced it up with my blueberry crêpes with crème fraîche and lemon curd, and a quiche Lorraine with ham, leeks, and gruyere." On the board, he wrote the new items in large letters.

Ingrid poked Flaxie. "Perhaps you should see that he gets a nice hot espresso."

"You could read Uncle Bernard like a book, Ingrid. I've seen the little things you do for him to adjust his humor. Have you yet had a good chat since he's been in Paris?"

"He's intent on his menu for the first tasting to take place today. He is a little frustrated, not locating his preferred ingredients like date purée, fennel oil from Italy, Peruvian purple cream, and a long list that I barely recall. Of course, he will improvise.

"He's accustomed to demanding whatever he needs and of course it magically appears. In Paris, he's been assigned a sous-chef that seems to have no intuition or efficiency and tends to prattle in a foreign language. I hope he makes a good impression as it would be hard for him to accept less than first place."

"That is what makes a great man into a great chef."

A Wenceslas Christmas 71

On Saturday morning, Flaxie was waiting for Logan on the valet veranda an hour before the opening of the boucher market at Chamonix.

The valet brought the delivery truck to the parking lot, a modified Vulcan open-back stake truck. It had been purchased second-hand when Flaxie was young, and she loved everything about it.

As a child, she had waited on Saturday mornings for her father, then climbed up beside him onto the worn green leather seat, watching him work the manual gears as they puttered downhill. Those were the days when she waved and called to every neighbor along the way, making it impossible to get to town without stopping and bartering along the route.

A fresh morning snowfall had blanketed the Alps, and the surface sparkled under the sunrise like a dusting of diamonds. This was the most beautiful time of the day with cable cars gliding over the glacier terrain. Ski lifts were active and all was right again at the Grand Marceau.

Rebounding from the ups and downs of the week, Flaxie was ready for the morning with Logan. Wearing a beige cable-knit sweater, khaki jodhpurs, sunglasses, and French cap, he appeared in her sight on the veranda.

"Over here, Logan"

In a plain navy dress with knit stockings and a woolen jacket with knee-high leather boots, he found her simplicity inviting and smiled his approval.

"This is the delivery truck?"

Flaxie tossed the keys to him and slid onto the passenger seat. "It's a family heirloom so drive her with care. You need to use the choke to get started, then expect one solid backfire before she revs up.

"A commercial parking lot near Place du Mont Blanc is close to the vendors, and our sturdy hand wagon is in the back. Most of the weekly produce, dairy, and meats are from the Savoie or Provence."

Flaxie ignored early screeching grinds of the gear as Logan found his way with the shift. She recalled a time when her father perched her on his knee. As hard as she tried, she was unable to coordinate the gear movement as her father pressed the clutch.

With a throaty putter, the truck ambled down the narrow mountain road, passing ancient medieval town castles, with turrets decked with festive lights and decorations.

Then over quaint cobbled streets, they meandered along canals and over stone bridges with a background of ancient cathedral spires rising above rooftops, accenting eons of history.

"The shopping won't be as daunting as you might expect," Flaxie said. "We have a weekly standing order for items like saucisson and magret de canard from La Maison. Seasonal fowl and duck are set aside for us at Platon. But for cheeses, so many unique textures get imported that you will want to sample them and make selections based on taste."

"I noticed we have escargot, scallops, salmon, and pâtés in the refrigeration. Where do they come from?"

"The seafood merchant delivers to the hotel on Mondays with scallops, salmon, turbot, perch, shrimps, and lobsters when in season, and specialties like oysters and urchins. Magnon will have sent a list based on your menus. You will have a standing Monday morning meeting."

For Logan, this was like a visit to a chef's amusement park, presenting a dilemma of delicacies to influence his selections and menu adjustments.

Flaxie stayed close, enjoying his temporary dependence on her. Seeing her, the vendors were overly friendly, especially recognizing the talented new chef they'd heard about at the Grand Marceau.

Madame Currier greeted him with a gracious nod. "Bonjour, Chef Powell. Please sample this newly arrived Reblochon, Sir, you'll find it exquisite. Also, I have a limited stock of eight-year aged ale-cheddar to accompany our sweet French leek mustard. It's excellent for charcuterie and Chef Marceau asks for it often."

After a tasting, Logan and Flaxie ordered ample stock for the holidays.

"One more thing," Logan said, "I'm looking specifically for a creamy-textured, fresh, local goat cheese. It seems the goats vary by region as does the uniqueness of the flavors."

Madame smiled wryly. "My brother sells at Les Houches and I wrested a small supply from him earlier this morning. You are correct, Monsieur Powell, the clover pasture is the best. Your hotel has its meadows up on the slopes where you have goats and honey in the summer and autumn."

Logan raised his brow and looked at Flaxie for confirmation. The chagrin on her face confirmed her error for not preparing him with that knowledge.

"Merci, Madame Currier," he continued. "Yes, we will gladly take some of your brother's goat cheese if you can spare some."

Next, they sampled a selection of sausage and dried meats until Logan was satisfied.

"Before we leave, Logan, we must visit a charming Italian delicatessen in the alley near the bridge. She has wonderful purées, foie gras, lobster pâtés, and rich olive oils."

"Lead the way as I wouldn't want to miss that."

Flaxie toted her share of the purchases back and forth

filling the wooden crates in the truck.

"This was a nice morning, Logan." She had a slight flush but looked directly into his eyes. "I want to say that I'm sorry if I've been somewhat difficult the last few days."

"No apology is necessary. We have both made alterations under these circumstances. Surely, you miss your uncle and it can't be easy to see me trying to take his place."

"Oh, you could never take his place, Logan, but there's room here for a good friendship."

"I'm still not sure when you are teasing me or insulting me. Which is it?"

Her gaze had the same pained longing as the night of the altercation with Hunter.

"You can trust me, Flaxie. I haven't known you long enough to understand fully what you have been through, but I would never hurt you or let anyone else."

"Thank you, Logan. I owe you an explanation."

On a bench near the market, she elaborated about the tragic death of her parents and how people and events still trigger memories.

"Nothing has anything to do with Hunter, he just had bad timing in asking me to the gala. I know it is planned that you will be returning to Paris by that time, but . . ."

Logan drew her close and hugged her, then kissed the top of her head before releasing his grip. This new sense of belonging confused him.

"We should get going, Logan. We're not done with our marketing. On the way back there are three farmhouses we'll stop at for local berries and herbs."

The truck chugged two miles uphill to an ambling, two-hundred-year-old stone farmhouse with four Guernseys in the yard, a trio of goats, and a Bernese.

A Wenceslas Christmas

"Here, this is Grandpa Louis' place," she said. "Just pull in by the barn."

"Grandpa Louis?"

"It's a friendly term—everyone calls him that. Our families have known each other for generations."

A jolly woman was attending to the fire at an outdoor, brick bread oven when the Vulcan pulled in. Across the yard, her linens flapped in the gentle breeze on an old-fashioned clothesline.

Louis himself was returning from furrowing with a hand plow and brimmed with a toothless smile. The aimless goats felt the need to close in and nibble on Logan's jacket.

The farmer's wife rushed to them like they were lost children. "Flaxie, it's so good to see you." Logan braced himself.

"Bonjour, Bonjour!" Louis boomed. "I have baskets of wild berries fresh from the countryside. Mostly blueberry and gooseberry, but some currants, wild chives, and even morels."

Logan was pleased with the offering. "This is exceptional and most appreciated."

Madame urged the couple to her late-season herb garden behind the barn. "Take whatever you like—there's fragrant rosemary fragrant and a choice of basil, some sweet and some tart. Chef Marceau always likes my leeks. Bernard and his father and before that his grandfather have come to my gardens. I also have pickled capers, some pretty pansies, and edible flowers for presentation."

Logan did his best to please Louis and his wife. "Certainly you have earned the family's seal of approval. I'll take whatever you can spare."

With two more stops, they arrived at the back loading bay of the Grand Marceau. The ringing of a bell brought out staff to unload the shipment, and when the truck was empty, Logan looked for Flaxie, but she was nowhere in sight.

Ingrid intercepted Flaxie as she carried parcels from the dock to the larder.

"Hallo, Flaxie! A beautiful bouquet delivery awaits you at the front desk. It's lovely with those gerberas you like, freesia, and even roses."

Flaxie's expression indicated her irritation.

"For heaven's sake, dear, I've never seen a woman troubled at receiving flowers," Ingrid said.

She whispered, "I'm guessing they are from Ranger Bodine, and I'm not interested. Ingrid, please have a look. If it's from the ranger, enjoy them yourself. Otherwise, I'd be glad to go and collect them myself."

"Oui, my dear. I'm sorry that I have caused you grief. Perhaps there is an alternative."

Flaxie stopped to listen. "Go ahead, Ingrid."

"Old Mrs. Thompson, you know the lady that comes every year by herself. She used to come with her husband to celebrate the season, and in the early years, her children came as well. Now there is only her. I go out of my way to make sure she attends our events and special meals—I'm sure the flowers would brighten her day."

"That's a beautiful thought. Mother would have done the same."

"Yes, it is alright to talk about your mother. She loved the Christmas season and embraced everyone. Your father as well. Do you remember choosing the great tree with him? The wounds heal more easily if you share them with others you love. They would want that for you."

"Thank you, Ingrid. I'd forgotten that you know me so well. It was you who helped me over the years and you kept

Uncle Bernard from falling apart. It is very true, I must work harder at embracing the season."

"Flaxie, we all lost the same people and each has pain differently. I know you loved them dearly, but you do not betray your parents to make room in your heart for another."

Turning away, Flaxie's shoulders shook as she allowed her grief to overtake her.

"Come with me, Flaxie. We need a little mother and daughter talk and a nice espresso before dinner preparations. Before your uncle left, I made a special request. If you are ready, I'd like to take you for a visit to your home."

Stunned, Flaxie stiffened up and her face bloomed with anticipation.

"Oh, Ingrid, do you really mean that we can go and it will be alright with Uncle."

With a lump on her throat, Ingrid's eyes pooled, seeing Flaxie's heartfelt joy.

10

The Food Critic

Logan was absorbed in the evening meal preparation and rehearsing the recitation in his mind when Flaxie bounded toward him.

When he looked up to see her, she saw something different. His face brightened as she hadn't seen before.

He's glad to see me.

Flaxie started talking a mile a minute with exhilaration. "Logan, er Chef Powell, I just checked the reservation list for tonight."

"Excellent, Flaxie." He continued to work as he listened.

"But wait . . . Are you familiar with the critique journal, 'The Epicurean Reviewer'? . . . Monsieur Damien Chouinard from Geneva? I read one of his articles once—he is a tough sell."

"What is this about, Flaxie?"

Her eyes were wide, midway between elation and fear.

"I'm sure it's him. He's dining with three other guests tonight. You know what this means?"

The dawn of realization blanketed Logan as his eyes darted to the menu, then to the prep area and the staff, all in slow motion.

Mon Dieu . . . Damien Chouinard, I know who that is. He can ruin me in two sentences. No, no. I won't let that happen. I'll remain calm for everyone.

"What table are they at?"

"Sixteen. Four people at 7 p.m."

His voice was relaxed. "We can't take any chances. Flaxie. You and Ingrid, do a meticulous review of the dining area and recheck every wait station. Every detail must be perfect. If you need help, ask Monsieur Dion for one of the concierges, but don't let on to him what this is about. The food critics are supposed to arrive in anonymity.

"However since the ambiance is part of the critique, have the maître d' reallocate any large groups or families with young children to tables further away. And ensure the freshest arrangements and candles are set out."

Sworn to secrecy, the staff was put on alert to pull together as a united team. The staff's pre-sampling buffet proceeded slowly with every bite savored and evaluated for any criticism to report in the seasonings.

At 6:45 p.m., Magnon announced that Table Sixteen was being cleared for the next seating. Measurements were visually taken of the placement of each glass according to its contents, the degrees of polished silverware awaiting their placement, and the crispness of linens and napkins.

A crush of personnel peered tactfully through the serving door peephole to spy on the goings-on in the dining room.

"Would you recognize Chouinard, Flaxie?"

On her cell phone, she opened a picture from his bylines.

"Of course, we don't know when this photo was taken."

Logan's phone buzzed with a text from Monsieur Dion. "Chouinard party has been delivered to the front door!"

He didn't know how Monsieur Dion learned of the staff secret but smiled with irritation and gratefulness.

Logan announced, "Bird's in the nest."

The head waiter took charge of the entourage, welcoming Monsieur Chouinard without showing preference. The group had one other portly middle-aged gentleman and two mature ladies wearing fashionable arrogance.

Ice water was delivered on cue, followed promptly by the sommelier with a comprehensive list of aperitifs and wines. Logan was relieved that the visit coincided with the hotel's regular Saturday night duet of harpists that performed soft classical music from a small stage.

Opting for a five-course dinner, each member of the epicureans ordered different selections with starters of black truffle soup under puff, foie gras de canard drizzled with passionfruit sauce, classic escargot in garlic butter, and featured truffle bomb croquette nestled on sweet shrimp, sea urchin, and caviar.

The second course presented tantalizing grenobloise salmon spears with pickled caper sauce over wilted greens, seared scallops, and pickled quail eggs. Two baskets of specially selected loaves of bread and focaccia slices were placed on the table with a sampling of herbed cheese butter and a fresh mountain creamery butter.

With Logan occupied with cooking and presentation, Flaxie monitored the progress at the table from a reasonable distance.

"Chouinard is jotting a lot of notes in his black book. It's hard to tell their reactions to the food, as they keep sampling one another's. Ah yes, the woman on his right stole his last bite, rude but a compliment to us."

"Excellent, Flaxie," Logan said. "We will do our best . . . that is all that Chef Marceau expects of us. However, he will be duly annoyed that the critic came knowing our Head Chef is at the Michelin competition in Paris. Chouinard must have known this. I'd be curious if he enquired when he made the reservation, knowing about the apprenticeship in place."

Did he ever write a review of Chef Augustus's award-winning shrimp stuffed cuttlefish in Paris? I wonder.

Marianne was keen to follow the conversation.

"Even if he did ask about you, Logan, your résumé is impeccable and you are an intriguing new competitor in a tight arena. If the review is spectacular, it is a feather in your cap. If not, it would reflect on Chouinard's judgment to usurp a Michelin star establishment in the absence of its head chef. That's just not done as a professional rule of etiquette."

"Turbot à la Normande with leek and spinach on Peruvian purple cream with mushrooms, mussels, and shrimp . . . is the champagne sauce ready for tasting?" Logan barked back to Marianne.

"Oui, Chef Powell."

Marianne passed him a tasting spoon with a sauce sample.

"Perfect, now the Citrus Poulet. The date purée is ready. I need the green olive gel then the fennel, cauliflower, and sweet potato mash," he demanded without hesitation. "The other two dishes with the Coquilles Saint-Jacques and pheasant à l'orange are warming. Make sure all plates are the same temperature when you serve them."

Wiping his hands, Logan watched the four servers parade the silver covered tureens to the critic's table. Admiring him, Flaxie put a reassuring hand on his back.

"We did well, chef!"

"Dessert servings will be ready next—Juliette's Savarin Baba au Rhum and the petite warm chocolate cake with apricot brandy sauce, crêpes suzette with Grand Marnier, and our flaming cherries jubilee for a spectacular finish."

"If my eyes don't deceive me, the woman next to Chouinard is smiling. I swear she came in as a dour and determined fault-finder. My word, she just ran her finger over the last of the brandy sauce for the last taste."

Logan halted their silent applause. "No celebrating until the last crumble of cheese is eaten and the final sip of port is consumed."

Ingrid rushed to join their preliminary celebration. "Good food overcomes, even for the harshest critic! They've been here for more than two hours. Logan, once the coffee and chocolate are out, why don't you go and celebrate. With Marianne, Magnon, Cobb, and Juliette, we can finish up here."

Time froze for an instant when Logan looked at Flaxie. She glowed with pride but searched his eyes for his answer.

"Yes, Ingrid, we'll accept your offer," he said with a wink.

As patrons dribbled out toward the discos and shuttles to the village street dancing, Flaxie stood to wait in the main foyer for Logan.

Now in a fitted black dress and with her hair twisted and clipped in a loose bouffant, she didn't look like the Flaxie that Logan was used to seeing rushing through the dining room.

"You look beautiful, Flaxie!"

He leaned in to kiss her cheek as a customary greeting but lingered at the scent of her seductive perfume. Instead of pulling back, he slipped his arm around her waist tightly.

She looked quizzically into his eyes and leaned into him.

A Wenceslas Christmas 83

"Where would you like to go?"

"We've earned a celebration but the beat from the disco is more than I'm ready for. However, the wine lounge on the mezzanine has a view over the mountains and Chamonix. The music is soft and classical and we can talk."

With her hand gently in his, Logan led her toward the elevator.

Settled by a fireplace with a view, Logan ordered champagne. As the server poured, they watched in silence as the bubbles rose.

He lifted his glass. "It's appropriate that we toast to our friendship, don't you think?"

Her eyes glazed, searching for something more. She had come to trust him implicitly in a short time, but he held a barrier between them.

"I've told you about my past, Logan, but I don't think you've said much about yours."

"I'm guilty of focusing on my career to a fault. I've dreamed of being a pivotal component in an establishment achieving a Michelin star or more. It's every chef's ultimate reality that, for me, has been unattainable.

"My parents sent me on a vacation in Europe after my graduation and I became invested in the gastronomic industry. I spent three years in London at Cordon Bleu and the Covent Market Academy."

He turned away with a sudden sadness. "I met a beautiful girl from Holland and we made plans together, but it wasn't my fate."

Flaxie saw the pain in his eyes and was beyond curious for Logan to explain, but she waited patiently.

He spoke in partial sentences, regaining composure every few seconds. "The bombing in the London subway . . ."

"I'm sorry, Logan, I can't imagine the pain you have been through." She wanted to reach for his hand to console him but waited for encouragement.

"Perhaps you understand very well. It must have been worse to lose parents at that age, who loved and raised you. Brigitte was only in my life for two short years, but I became determined not to put myself in a position to endure such pain again."

Flaxie searched for the right words to equate comfort. "I am consoled by old Elvis records in my room and sometimes I feel that this is my heartbreak hotel—it's my home, my castle, and my prison. I'll always be an orphan and sometimes I became bitter that I never siblings to share memories with."

As soon as she said it, she regretted the words.

"Oh, dear Flaxie, this could never be a prison, and you mustn't think like that. It's a magnificent place filled with charm that provides joy and memories for those that come here. I'm going to work on changing your perspective. I came looking for an answer to my dream, hoping I could succeed in persuading Chef Marceau to keep me.

"Instead, I found the most unique, caring group of people, a paradise of alpine scenery, and an opportunity to make each day better for all those fortunate enough to arrive at the Grand Marceau. Regardless of my tenure, I plan to make an impression here that the hotel won't forget for a long time."

"I am very glad that you came, Logan. I was thinking of something a wise woman said to me recently. Ingrid and my uncle are a love story of their own, but complicated as only my uncle doesn't realize it. The other day, she reminded me that someday soon, Uncle Bernard will realize that his guardian angel is standing right here beside him. I've been

A Wenceslas Christmas

blinded and have done nothing to play cupid. I have a responsibility to play a role in their future when he returns."

Logan brightened with amusement at the revelation.

"Instead of waiting until your uncle returns from Paris, you should look at who's across the table from you."

Slowly he reached his hand to hers.

"The best of life is now, don't keep waiting for something in the future. We've both had too much heartache and sorrow in life. I can't believe it is me speaking these words, but being here, I've realized how precious today is."

11

Marceau in Paris

Flaxie skipped into the Monday morning meeting that was already underway with discussions of Christmas festivities, special dinners, brunches, and buffets. Menus from the past two years were scattered on the table.

Logan's eyes lit up and watched her every movement as he continued with his patter.

"Welcome, Mademoiselle Marceau, we're glad that you could join us. I presume you had reason to sleep in."

Flaxie replied flippantly and enjoyed toying with the moment. "Yes, I had a very good reason."

She waved a document in the air.

"It's here, the critic review is here!" She giggled with pleasure seeing Logan's face.

All eyes went to her as the room hushed. Logan didn't move.

"Go ahead, read it!"

"Byline of Monsieur Damien Chouinard of the Gastronomic Reviewer of Geneva.

"At this festive season, our gastronomical fans have eyes on the international chef's competition at the King George hotel in Paris. The greatest chefs from across Europe will be on-site to demonstrate their ultimate skills. Among those invited is the renowned Chef Bernard Marceau who hails from generations of chefs and hoteliers in the alpine hills at Mont Blanc above Chamonix.

"Rather than bore you with the tedious menus and recipes being produced in Paris, I took my guests to the Grand Marceau to see how such an iconic hotel would fare at Christmas while their famous chef Marceau was receiving accolades among the top five chefs in the competition.

"A daring choice for Chef Marceau to hand the reins to a relatively unknown sous-chef formerly of the King George itself who has not yet been among the list of Michelin contributors. Logan Powell, the sous-chef, surprised my party with a spectacular and succulent meal.

"Our appetizer choices were not particularly unusual, however, the presentation and blend of flavors excelled. Each plate was introduced with a creative presentation and always a tantalizing taste of a secret ingredient that I was not able to define.

"He goes on to list every item. You'll want to read the detailed description later. But I'll continue.

"I would be remiss not to state the superb ambiance of the dining room from a magical lyre duet to the fragrances of Christmas pine. The bread basket was unique and we devoured every piece flavored with fresh, house-made creamery-herbed

cheese beurre.

"Four were in our party and we chose a five-course dinner. The appetizers were a tantalizing blend of new flavors with the presentation surprising, from truffle croquette with caviar to cuttlefish stuffed with shrimp mousse. As the main course was introduced, we each had the privilege to sample the other dishes including Turbot à la Normande, citrus poulet, Coquilles Saint Jacques, and an inventive pheasant a l'orange. Ordinarily, I would calculate excessive salt or garlic or have some criticism but none could be found.

"Our meal was delivered timely over an hour and a half giving us time to appreciate each course. The waiter heartily suggested we enjoy the Savarin Baba au Rhum at the conclusion. My female companion was partial to chocolate and chose the warm chocolate cake with apricot and brandy sauce, then we sampled a spectacular Crêpe Suzette and a flaming cherries jubilee, a delightful tingle at the end of an incredible meal. I would have regretted not tasting these amazing desserts.

"Since my presence and critiques at dining establishments are intended to be anonymous, I did not present myself to the hotel staff or the chef, Logan Powell, who has a Bachelor of Culinary Arts from London's Cordon Bleu and training at the London Academy. Powell was highly recommended by Chef Augustus of the King George in Paris.

"I will return with full intentions of giving my profuse compliments to an intriguing up and coming chef apprentice onto the European gastronomic forum.

"If you are looking for a charming holiday, I would recommend a few days in the alpine villages of Mont Blanc. If you are fortunate to find a sought after reservation at the Grand Marceau, it would be well worth the investment. I am rarely wrong in my speculations and foresee a brilliant future here with Marceau and Powell with another Michelin star in the making.

Flaxie looked up to boisterous applause, directed at the chef. She stepped back beside Ingrid to give the staff opportunity to deliver congratulations.

Ingrid whispered, "Your uncle . . . and your father would be very proud of this moment. The next hurdle you have is how to hold on to him."

Flaxie continued to address the group. "You should all know that Bernard is in the first place group. We must see that he receives a copy of the review."

She spun around to Ingrid. "Please send a courier to Paris as soon as possible!"

The Monday meeting labored over assignments and Logan was fastidious ordering condiments and ingredients.

"We want this Christmas to be extraordinary. Since Chef Marceau is in Paris we are looking for a Father Christmas volunteer. If no one is eager, I will defer to Monsieur Dion to seek a recruit from his staff or outside services."

Ingrid added, "The great suit is upstairs, but as you could guess, we will need an amply sized substitute."

As Roberto Dion entered the kitchen to give his congratulations on the critique, all heads swung around to size up his physique in comparison to the suit.

Dion was flustered by the stares. "Why I only meant to offer my compliments on the incredible review, however, I feel I have intruded. I'll come back later."

Logan chortled, "Ah, Monsieur Dion, you've arrived precisely when we are discussing a critical need for a Father Christmas. The chair remains empty for the play and children's event and then again Christmas morning. Aren't you are a father yourself of two small children? I admire your humor and congeniality, perhaps you might consider it."

Dion postured like a peacock and blushed. "Me, as Father Christmas? Most certainly, I would be delighted."

With a smattering of applause, Dion retreated with a bounce in his step, practicing his 'ho, ho, ho'.

Word of the delectable success of Chef Powell quickly leaked out among the staff and down into Chamonix, bringing a stream of well-meaning congratulations.

That evening, a courier's bicycle arrived at avenue de George, near the Champs-Élysées in Paris. Snapping his fingers, a bellhop appeared immediately to be of service to the delivery boy.

"Take this directly to Chef Marceau, the jolly chef with the white beard, in the Versailles dining room. There is a break in the conference for a few hours."

Bernard was surprised to receive the envelope and concerned that something might be amiss at the Grand Marceau to be suitable for this interruption.

"Ah, it is my Ingrid's writing on the sleeve."

He carefully slit the end and pulled out the letter and the review. A wave of homesickness was fleeting. He read then re-read the review before sighing, then threw his head back and bellowed a hearty chuckle.

"I am indeed a proud Papa. Ingrid was right, the young sous-chef deserved his chance and has proven himself worthy of the Grand Marceau."

Rarely did Marceau indulge in a glass of wine while he was refining his gourmet artistry, however, this was an occasion to make a toast.

"To Chef Logan Powell!"

The celebration was brief as a bell boy found him with a hand-written telephone message. It was from Benoit Willoughby, the barristers' firm on the Champs-Élysées.

A Wenceslas Christmas

"Yes, the time has come. I'll go to their offices in the morning to set the wheels in motion. Benoit and Milton will be relieved to see me."

The exhilaration and inspiration that Bernard enjoyed since arriving in Paris were new to him. However, the comradery among the other participants had elements of strain like inventors protecting their patents.

The King George Hotel was elegantly adorned with magnificent trees that lined the corridors, each with glistening lights that sparkled like stars, and golden baubles and ornaments.

At intervals, a caroling troupe in early century costumes strolled through the public areas in harmonies of old Christmas classics.

It's not truly Christmas unless I'm at home with my family. Family . . . that's what is missing here. The guests are snobby and hardly a child is in sight. And where's Father Christmas?

Bernard recalled Ingrid's face when he gave his farewells in the hotel lobby.

"Life will not return to normal after this."

She had looked into his soul when she said perhaps they could have a spring visit to Paris.

Why would she say something like that?

Then an idea struck him like a thunderbolt.

I have been such a fool. My soulmate has been right there beside me for twenty years. How could I not have seen that my reliance on her and my delight to see her every day was not friendship, but was so much deeper? Here I am, a middle-aged chef searching for my dream when everything I want in life is at home . . . with Ingrid. I know this. She is the love of my life.

Within a few minutes, the clatter of pots and pans

invaded his intimate space and the vision of Ingrid.

"Bonsoir, Chef Marceau, here are the choices for tonight's dinner."

Augustus marched with his arms oscillating, and an underling followed closely on his heels, dispatching a printed list of appetizers, entrees, and desserts.

"Make whatever modifications needed to the ingredients to accentuate your feature. Be precise with your notations."

Bernard looked Augustus in the eye wondering if he was aware of Chouinard's review. He saw nothing more than insolence and was relieved.

12

Secrets of the Great Book

After the Monday meeting dispersed, Magnon answered a knock at the receiving bay to accept the supply of the week's produce, poultry, meats, and seafood. It was Louis, the affable farmer from the hillside.

"Hallo, is Chef Powell available?"

"Come in Louis, come in . . . Juliette will fix you up with a special coffee and he selected sweets and pastries. Of course, take some home for your family."

Logan meandered over, delighted to see the visitor. "What brings you to the Grand Marceau this morning?"

"On the weekend I was game hunting up in the Alps with my brother and my sons. We were looking for pheasant and partridge, but we crossed paths with an angry wild boar. She is large and hanging in my barn. My wife suggested I offer the loins to you for your Christmas menu.

"As it happens we had the Duke with us, my coonhound.

He has an envious scent to seek out black truffles from evergreen oak roots. The truffles from each region in France vary in flavor and I believe these to be the most superb."

Louis was nervous making his offer, and at last, he drew a black knobby clump from his pocket.

"So kind of you to think of me, Louis."

Logan rubbed his chin while his eyes went blank considering the sausage and apricot stuffing and tying the loin ribs with festive gold crowns. Accepting the black clump, he closed his eyes and sniffed to savor the precious aroma.

"I'd be delighted to accept your hunting spoils. Shall I send someone to collect it, or would you bring it here?"

"Oh, my sons will bring it."

Louis' eyes wandered to Juliette's baking, with the warm, new relationship pleasing Logan as he relished the opportunity to build a rapport in the community.

"Help yourself and I will join you for espresso. Of course, you normally send a bill to the hotel for your services, correct?"

At his sight, Flaxie edged her way nearer. "Is there room for one more?"

She squeezed another bistro chair up to the large table. "This sugar-crusted brioche with homemade currant jelly is the best. Sophia and your boys will enjoy it too."

As Louis puttered away in his truck, Flaxie spontaneously put her arm around Logan's shoulder and planted a kiss on his cheek. She didn't care what Marianne or any of the others thought.

"This is a good day, Chef!"

Keeping a poker face, he looked at Marianne as her jaw dropped in shock at the unexpected affection between the two. She knew him too well and he gave in to a smile and a wink.

Logan retreated to the great book in Marceau's office thumbing for a particular page—a recipe and description for wild boar.

Enthralled by sketches and notations, he didn't notice that time was ticking away until Ingrid tapped on the open door.

"I sent the review to Bernard in Paris and he telephoned with his congratulations. He couldn't be more proud than if he had trained you personally. You know the two of you are of like minds and would be quite the duo."

"We can't always have what we wish for. Chef Marceau will be returning at the end of next week and I'll pack my bags and plan to return to my daily routine in Paris."

Ingrid looked wistfully at him.

"It doesn't sound like you're looking forward to that. You know if you want something badly you have to try very hard. I might be able to press my influence into Bernard's thinking about continuing the protégé arrangement, but I would not set about such a ruse without encouragement."

"You'd do that for me?" Logan said in amazement.

"First you must understand my role in this family. I watch over Flaxie to see that she finds happiness and I also make appropriate suggestions, as necessary, to Bernard who has my heart so that he stays focused and on course."

"I see that your proposal is somewhat of a package deal to look after your family."

"Just a suggestion, Logan, take some time to think about it . . . but don't wait too long."

"Ingrid, you have been kind to me. After schooling, I wandered around Europe intending to be a chef in one of the finest establishments. It's been years since I had anyone care about my dreams—your words mean a great deal."

"Sometimes fate leads us to where we are supposed to be in life. That's the exact feeling I had when I faced Flaxie's father Frederick and his father twenty years ago. I was intimidated but I knew it was in my hands to change their minds."

"Ingrid, from what Flaxie tells me, you are *not* underappreciated, but you're adored. I once had a fiancé and then one day it was too late, fate took her from me. Regret is the hardest emotion to deal with."

Ingrid forced an understanding smile, hiding a pensive feeling of sadness and hurt.

Tour groups were lined in the lobby, with a queue of registering guests extending to the center Christmas tree. For children and families, Ernesto and his helpers organized toboggan runs, skating parties, and hayrides for the day.

Hunter Bodine advised that the red flag would be up until the alpine crew had thoroughly inspected the upper ridge, as a heavy snowfall had come in overnight. Throughout the valley, Hunter was respected for his commitment to safety and the alpine environment.

He spotted Flaxie who was discussing the guest overflow with Dion.

"Bonjour, Flaxie et Monsieur Dion." His eyes were only looking at her, hoping for a truce.

"What brings you here this morning, Hunter?" she asked.

He pulled a dozen warning posters from an envelope. "Please post these, Flaxie. We put up the red flag but I'm sure it won't be for long. A small avalanche swept over the Grand Montets already and our people will stay on the scene for safety. I'll take a run with the dog sled this afternoon. In a crisis we're always short on staff."

A Wenceslas Christmas

Flaxie's reaction softened. "Hunter, thanks for watching over us and our guests."

"Also, I want to congratulate Logan and the staff for the food critic's review. Everyone in the village is talking about it. You must be proud of him for this compliment."

"We are indeed honored, but it took our entire crew to make it happen. I've never properly thanked you, Hunter, for saving him on Mont Blanc that first day. He has become a valuable member of the Grand Marceau."

The words stung Hunter. Although he had eyes for Flaxie for a long time, it wasn't until Logan was the competition that he stepped up.

"Flaxie, I owe you an apology for my behavior. I wouldn't intentionally offend you or make you fearful of me."

His eyes lowered and he shifted feet. "It's clear that you're interested in someone else. I promise to step aside and wish you the best."

As he struggled to make the best of a bad situation, Flaxie softened in sympathy.

"I appreciate the sentiment, Hunter. Can we put any misunderstandings behind us and go on like old friends as we have for years?"

They both knew it would never be the same again.

Logan loomed over the Christmas menus and sought out Marceau's recipes for the traditionally roasted goose with truffle chestnut dressing.

Once more he noticed the yellowed envelope.

"Ingrid mentioned Flaxie's birthday. I must ask her when that is. Something significant is associated with her 25th and worthy enough to involve lawyers, not just local lawyers but a prestigious firm in Paris."

As he stuffed the envelope back into place, the last few

loose pages of the book drew his attention, blueprints, and old yellowed artists' etchings from December 2000, of a new chalet called 'Mistletoe Lodge'.

Studying the specifications, he quickly realized it was for land on the rise behind the Grand Marceau.

Guilt overcame him for spying on Bernard Marceau's personal affairs, and he cinched up the strap and returned the great book to its place.

Flaxie makes me want to seek the best in life. If she knew that I'd uncovered this information, she might think I see her for her inheritance and not purely for the person I love.

Ainsley Hayhurst, a late twenties lad with straggly hair, sat at an outdoor café on the Champs-Élysées perusing the daily news, searching for the gourmet competition results at the King George hotel.

Finding it, he muttered aloud, "Ah, Bernard Marceau . . . I will look forward to meeting you."

He picked up a worn portfolio artist's case and headed off toward the bus terminal. After studying the schedules, he paid with euro coins for a pass.

It was Wednesday morning when Bernard Marceau rose in his Paris suite. The schedule for today was light and he didn't need to confer with conference officials until 11 a.m. Given the break, he phoned the office of Willoughby & Singleton for an appointment.

Searching his through his valise from Mont Blanc, he realized he had forgotten to retrieve the envelope about Flaxie's 25th birthday.

"Willoughby knows the situation well enough, I'll have to rely on his documents. I can't believe that it's been twenty years since father passed away. He was the picture of good health with enough ambitions for a full lifetime. Although his time was cut short with a heart attack, he lived a good life. Soon after that, Frederick and Francesca perished and mother took a stroke."

Bernard rationalized to ease his guilt. "It was a great deal to endure but I had Flaxie to think of. Not wanting to bring her pain, I decided not to discuss these legal details. I should have told her when she turned 18."

Wearing a dark brown business suit, he donned a wool chapeau top hat and tucked an umbrella under his arm. As he prepared to exit the brass doors, the desk clerk called him.

"Monsieur Marceau, there is a courier delivery for you here. The gentleman said that it is urgent."

Ripping through the levels of concealment, Bernard found a hand-written letter.

Dear Chef Marceau,

I read that you were in Paris for a cooking test. To be blunt, I uncovered information that my mother was your sister-in-law, Francesca Stanhope. I was born out of wedlock before she married your brother Frederick, and given up for adoption. I'm a starving artist living in Montparnasse and when I heard you were in town, I thought we could meet.

Signed: Ainsley Hayhurst

"Incredulous! Willoughby can deal with this."

Choosing to take a brisk walk to the Champs-Élysées, he dismissed the valet's offer to wave a taxi.

"The day is much too lovely to ride in a car." Looking toward the Eiffel tower, he took a deep breath of fresh air and listened to the city sounds, satisfying his tourist duty.

Twenty minutes later, he entered the marbled hall of a prestigious office tower above the popular shopping district of Paris's main rue.

He addressed the main floor reception. "Monsieur Willoughby is expecting me. Bernard Marceau from Mont Blanc."

"Very well. Monsieur Willoughby's assistant will arrive momentarily to escort you. Please take a seat."

Instead, Marceau chose to pace back and forth in front of the glass wall looking out onto the street.

I've always kept my eyes on my task and neglected to see outside the box. Paris is a romantic city. Right outside this very door, a busker is playing his accordion to Ole Sole Mio.

His laugh was startling.

13

The Bequest

Willoughby's comment was pointed. "Bonjour, Bernard, I'm glad you were able to fit us into your schedule. I've been trying to contact you for months to get a start on things."

"Yes, yes, Benoit, but you must appreciate that we are in the midst of a festive season that taxes me to the limit. It was all I could do to tear myself away for this gourmet event that Ingrid and Flaxie insisted I would enjoy."

"I hope it is giving you great pleasure. I check on the daily results and see you're still in the winner's circle leading into the finale."

"Let's get to business, Benoit, as I must return soon to the kitchens and prepare myself."

Willoughby pulled out a thick file and laid it open on the desk. Peering over his glasses it was apparent that Bernard had come empty-handed.

The lawyer slid a writing case toward Marceau. "Do you wish me to read each document, or shall I summarize and you can take whatever notes you desire?"

"Please summarize it. I'm aware that Father's will left the entire estate to my brother and myself with the stipulation that my mother is cared for and given anything she wished."

"Yes, that's correct, and then there was the unfortunate death of Frederick three years later. Francine, or Flaxie as she is called affectionately, is the only heir of her parents. As such, her father's portion of the estate has been held in trust until her birthday which is coming up late in January."

"Correct," Marceau grunted, then hesitated. He pulled the letter from Ainsley from his pocket and turned it over and over in his hands with indecision.

"Your father was an astute man, as was his father, and the heritage of the Grand Marceau must remain in the family. Despite my insisting that your father give you, the eldest son, 51%, and Frederick 49% to enable future decisions to be made without legal challenge, he would not hear of it. Singleton assumed the interim voting shares for Flaxie and it seems everything has gone smoothly."

"My father was an honorable man and I agree with him," Marceau said.

"Well, then that brings us to the significant investments of the estate. Do you wish me to detail the assets or would you prefer to bring Francine back to go over it? She should be prepared to sign papers, having some knowledge of the estate."

"I suppose I should show you this. Its rubbish since Frederick and Francesca died together, she did not survive my brother to personally inherit the estate. This kid is not even Marceau blood, so there's no question of Flaxie's inheritance."

A Wenceslas Christmas

Willoughby frowned as he pored over the letter.

"This Hayhurst fellow has no legal foundation, however, you must consider that he is a maternal half-brother of Flaxie. It would be up to her if she decides to drop a settlement on him as a family matter."

"Yes, Benoit, I'd neglected that viewpoint. You're right, I should have come sooner."

Marceau sighed. "Frankly, Benoit, may I talk to you on a personal level. You can see how this is awkward for me."

"Of course, Bernard, we are old friends."

"You see, I have a dear friend that has been by my side at the hotel for all these years, even before father died. My time in Paris has been a godsend in that I have been able to clear my head. When I get back to the Grand, I intend to propose to Ingrid."

"I'm delighted for you, Bernard. I have always said to my wife that one day cupid's arrow will get its mark. It's been an obvious match for years."

Bernard nodded. "That wasn't so hard after all but there's more. I have talked with Ingrid on the phone and she thinks that Flaxie has fallen in love with the sous-chef. My family has always believed that love comes before money, I don't want this inheritance to ruin a future for Flaxie, to neither encourage nor discourage a match."

"My dear friend, I can consult with legal matters, but with matters of the heart, you will have to rely on your niece. The inheritance can simply continue in investment funds with a living allowance, then board meetings, and annual reviews. Otherwise, life should go on.

"The only other critical decision will be regarding the land set aside for Mistletoe Lodge."

"Yes, the lodge. It suddenly seems very appropriate."

Bernard looked at his pocket watch and began to rise

from his chair.

"Oh no, Bernard, we're not finished. I have prepared papers that you need to sign for us to begin transferring ownership and funds from the trust."

"Very well, if you insist."

With an attempt at humor, Willoughby added, "However, if you assure me that you'll return with Flaxie soon, I will call the guards off the door."

Half an hour later, Marceau strode along the shopping district with a lighter step, a smirk on his face, and an occasional guffaw then came to an abrupt stop in front of Tiffany's.

Immediately on Bernard's departure, Willoughby conferred with his partner, Milton Singleton, about the upcoming visit to Mont Blanc.

"Milton, I have harbored Frederick Marceau's secret for many years."

He rotated a sealed envelope in his hands.

"This has been in our safety deposit box. He was desperately in love with Francesca and wanted to ensure her secret was not revealed, that before he met her she had a child out of wedlock. The boy taken from her at the convent was adopted by a good family. However, Frederick and Francesca's good conscience provided for a small inheritance to be set aside should the child ever seek out his birth mother. Oddly, it seems that this is the same fellow that has turned up now, Ainsley Hayhurst."

"Most definitely, Benoit," Singleton said. "To keep matters at arms-length perhaps it would be best if I made contact myself and see the boy's motives."

The next afternoon, Ainsley Hayhurst slunk into the elevator to Willoughby & Singleton's offices on the Champs-

Élysées. He had a blond, curly crop and wore an ill-fitting designer jacket and trendy flat cap. He nervously pressed the button for Willoughby's floor knowing he'd have to face scrutiny.

"Bonjour, Monsieur Hayhurst, we have been awaiting your arrival. Tell us what brings you here."

"My adopted mother told me on her death bed who my birth mother was and gave me the address here in Paris. It seems Francesca married into a well-to-do family that owns the Grand Marceau on Mont Blanc.

"I'm well aware that she died many years ago. When I was young, my adopted father split from my mother and she struggled to put me through university. My passion, however, was to be an artist."

Singleton bit his tongue as he listened.

"Monsieur Hayhurst, I hope you are aware that since Francesca's death was simultaneous to her husband's, there wouldn't be any Marceau money directed to you. However, I have here a hand-written request from Frederick Marceau that you be given a reasonable sum as a good-will gesture.

"You realize, of course, the Marceau's were not aware of your adoption details or your whereabouts these many years. The birth was handled at the convent and the family knew little of your existence."

"I understand how this might appear, Monsieur Willoughby, but it is natural that when the family you have known to be yours is gone, anyone would seek out their blood relationship. Would it be possible to arrange a meet with my half-sister?"

Willoughby and Singleton looked at each other. "As it happens we will be conducting business in Mont Blanc after New Year's. Leave it with us and we'll let you know if something can be arranged."

Ainsley left the attorney's offices feeling distressed. Sauntering onto a side street a good walk from the Champs-Élysées, he retrieved a large art portfolio from the bus locker. With his collar up to brave the cold wind, he stuck his hands into his pocket and headed toward the artists' hill in Montmartre to sell his paintings.

The phone rang in Marceau's room at the King George while he was examining the documents. He picked up the receiver to hear Benoit's voice.

"Bernard, the Hayhurst lad seems to be on the up and up. If you would like us to continue as a buffer in this matter, an introduction could be possible when Singleton and I come to Mont Blanc after New Year's.

"You'll be relieved to know that he was primarily interested in Flaxie as opposed to the settlement offer. I can obtain a photograph of the young fellow from the security camera if you would like to see what he looks like. He indeed has Francesca's blond curls as does Flaxie."

14

Good King Wenceslas

On Mont Blanc, a scurry of holiday activity surged at the Grand Marceau. Songsters in top hats and scarves, and hands in wool and fur muffs, strolled through the lobby and out to the skating rinks, chanting choruses of traditional carols.

An impromptu parade from the village was led by the dancing snowman mascot, with character alpine minstrels singing *'An Austrian went Yodeling'*, showing off their liveliest foot slapping and twirling.

Once an Austrian went yodeling on a mountain so high,
When he met with an avalanche interrupting his cry.
Ho-li-ah, ho-le-rah-hi-hi-ah,
Ho-le rah cuckoo (rumble, rumble sounds)
Ho-li-ah, ho-le-rah-hi-hi-ah,
Ho-le rah cuckoo (rumble, rumble sounds)

A picturesque team of yoked Clydesdales, with brushed, white furry hooves, pranced and snorted on the street, pulling sleigh wagons decked with red and green jingling bells, with drivers in Bavarian bundhosen and felt alpine hats.

Tonight would be the arrival of Father Christmas, to sit in the great chair by the hotel's center hall tree. Along the entrance lane, children stood high on their toes for the first glimpse or sound of the sleigh.

"Oh, Mama, I hear the bells coming," a young girl gasped. "There's Rudolph."

A cheer erupted from the bystanders, as coming over the bend was Roberto Dion, well-padded in brilliant red garb and reining four horses plodding in unison, with reindeer ears affixed to their heads.

"Ho, Ho, Ho! Ho, Ho, Ho!"

A roar echoed up and down the street to welcome Santa on his sleigh, with the cheers emanating through the lobby.

"Come, Logan, we have to see Father Christmas!" Flaxie's eyes danced like a child, that it was indeed the jolly red elf in person.

Logan swept up a box of gingerbread men and a bunch of carrots from the cooler and followed her to the portico.

He passed the bucket to Roberto who was transformed into his jolly role. As the sleigh passed, Logan ran alongside with Flaxie behind.

"Father Christmas!" he shouted. "I have treats for you and the reindeer. Merry Christmas!"

"This is wonderful. I'm having a grand time, better even than I'd imagined." Dion pointed to a woman with an infant and toddler. "See ahead there—my children and my Lilleth."

Flaxie tugged at Logan's coat as they jogged. "Either you get in with Santa or you stay with me."

A Wenceslas Christmas

"Have a jolly evening, I can't come with you as I have a beautiful lady waiting."

And as a passenger sleigh passed, he shouted, "Two more here . . . Ernesto, can you flag them over?"

He lifted Flaxie over the rudder, covered her legs with a blanket, and slipped in beside her.

"Christmas in the Alps is more romantic than those I've spent in Paris."

Looking into her eyes, he saw the magical delight of a child.

"I love it here," she said. "There's nothing like it. You've awakened a store of memories for me, Logan, some sad, but in the end it is good. I carried on my life at the hotel pretending to be a contented child, but the spirit of Christmas had been lost deep in my heart.

"Of course the three wise men don't represent Faith, Hope, and Charity, but those are the essence of what I am feeling now. My faith is in you and for the future. My heart wants to share with those not as fortunate."

As Logan pondered, Flaxie squeezed his arm waiting.

"At the end of every meal, the hotel has so much food left that spoils. Homeless or destitute people are not always visible in the village, but there's a hostel at the end of the street, and others are sheltered at the church. On Christmas Eve, we could deliver meals."

"A tremendous idea, Logan! And wait . . . gift bags too. The hotel has excess toiletry kits, teas, candy canes, hot chocolate packets, and we can top them up with chocolates and marzipans."

Her eyes had lit up imagining the joy it would bring.

"What inspired this, Logan?"

"It's a Christmas carol. I'm not a student of music, but I

understand the meaning of one in particular. I've always been touched by 'Good King Wenceslas'. He was a kind and incredible king, centuries ago in Prague."

Flaxie raised her eyebrows to bait him. "Sing it for me."

"You don't think that I'll do that," he bantered. "I'm not good with tunes but I know the lyrics by heart."

With her head on his shoulder, he spoke the rhyming words.

"Good King Wenceslas looked out
On the feast of Stephen,
When the snow lay round about,
Deep and crisp and even
Brightly shone the moon that night,
Though the frost was cruel,
When a poor man came in sight,
Gathering winter fuel.

"Hither, page, and stand by me.
If thou know it telling,
Yonder peasant, who is he?
Where and what his dwelling?
Sire, he lives a good league hence,
Underneath the mountain,
Right against the forest fence
By Saint Agnes fountain.

"Bring me flesh, and bring me wine.
Bring me pine logs hither.
Thou and I will see him dine
When we bear the thither.
Page and monarch, forth they went,
Forth they went together
Through the rude wind's wild lament
And the bitter weather.

"In his master's step he trod,
Where the snow lay dented.
Heat was in the very sod
Which the saint had printed.
Therefore, Christian men, be sure,
Wealth or rank possessing,
Ye who now will bless the poor
Shall yourselves find blessing.

"The last two lines sum it up, Flaxie. 'Ye who now will bless the poor shall yourselves find blessing'."

Flaxie stared at him in awe and applauded in her soft gloves. "Wow! I get it. And I believe I have discovered another act for the Christmas Eve show."

"Only if you do it with me."

Logan kissed her on the lips, then sat back looking satisfied. With a mischievous smirk, he whistled the Saint Wenceslas tune.

15

Logan's Plea

On the day before Christmas Eve, the time had come for Uncle Bernard's Christmas gift. Silently easing into the chef's office, Ingrid retrieved a ring of keys from Bernard's desk and went in search of Flaxie.

The pair met up near the foyer's great tree. "You're looking for me, Ingrid?"

"Yes, dear."

"Is everything alright, Ingrid? You look upset."

"Oh, everything is good, but I have an unusual request for you. Of course, you are free to decline."

"Certainly, what is it?"

"Your family apartment has been the source of pain for many years, but it's time to recover your memories and move on. Everything there is exactly as it was left."

Flaxie's hands clasped her cheeks in awe. "Oh, Ingrid, I'd love to see my home again. It would be the most wonderful present. When can we go?"

"After the noon luncheon if Logan can spare you."

Flaxie embraced her friend and held her lest the moment is lost. "I adore you, Ingrid."

She bounded into the kitchen to tell Logan.

"Ingrid and your uncle know you best. If this is the time, then you must be ready."

She looked at him with a deep soul-searching. His eyes didn't hide his loneliness and sadness.

"Logan, since you've been here, I am ready to move forward with my life, to grow up, take on responsibility. I want to build a future—I wouldn't be ready if you weren't a part of it. Please give me hope . . . hope this won't all come crashing to an end when Uncle Bernard returns."

"Thank you. I appreciate all of that." He didn't smile or take her in his arms, but troubled, he went to the office.

She's right, I can't just leave and go back to Paris. Too much has changed in my life, with too much to lose. I won't accept that I am powerless in my destiny.

Close to the lunch recitation, Logan still hadn't opened his door. Through the glass, it was apparent that he was on hold on a telephone call.

In these past days, he'd gone over the exact words he would say and now that the moment had come he was trying to prepare for the answer.

Without a courteous preamble, he blurted, "Hello, Chef Marceau! If you could spare a moment, Sir! I'd like you to consider keeping me on at the Grand as your apprentice. In your absence, I have become fond of this family and my impending return to Paris will complicate the future for your niece and me."

"Ha, ha, Logan, I understand well the matters of the

heart. I left a lovely pair of ears at the Marceau and she has kept me informed. I regret that I'm not there to see it for myself. I'm facing a dilemma affecting my future, as well, but I know what I must do. First, I congratulate you on your review with Chouinard. It was most impressive.

"I've had time to think about my prospects and this rigid routine in Paris has reinforced my view. We are at the same fork in the road, my son, however, I'm not ready to give up my head chef position in Mont Blanc. It is part of my lineage. Saying that, considering my age, a future change in marital status, then Flaxie's inheritance trust, I'm pleased to hear of your interest."

Logan was surprised and relaxed by Marceau's openness and he sensed reason for hope.

"Should it be possible for me to remain, I will need to give my resignation to Chef Augustus and Director Morningside very soon. Of course, if this cannot be immediate, I will return to the King George until you decide on any arrangement."

"Logan, you have made my future easier with your suggestion. However, you realize that I am a guest here hosted by the hotel and would not want to make my presence uncomfortable. The Piece de Resistance will be on Christmas Day when the final awards are announced, then I will be free to return.

"However, Logan, you are slotted back in here as a sous-chef on the 29th. It would be fair to your employer to give reasonable notice as I would expect from any employee. Perhaps you could give me a day to think this over and I'll call you regarding my decision."

Bernard lingered on the line to say something else. "Logan, since I've been here I've heard a few things. I know about the signature dish that Chef Augustus submitted, the

A Wenceslas Christmas

one that you created. I would understand how a colleague of mine might not see his future in this establishment. Let me mull over a few thoughts."

"That would be more than fair, Chef Marceau. In the meantime, Ingrid and Flaxie send their congratulations and are looking forward to seeing you."

Hearing more hesitation, Logan waited for Marceau to end the call.

"Logan, does it frighten you that Flaxie will receive a large inheritance? If it doesn't, you are not right for her. On the other hand, if it does, let your heart lead over your fear. I could tell you a love story about my brother and his wife and you would know the answer to your dilemma."

"I appreciate your advice, Sir. If the opportunity presents itself, I would thoroughly enjoy more life lessons."

Ingrid was waiting not far from the door with her arms folded. At last, he opened the door. Searching his eyes, it was apparent that a pivotal decision was pending.

"It's like jumping into the rapids, Logan. Focusing on your destination makes it easier, otherwise, you can flounder and put yourself in peril. You can choose not to jump, or you can take a leap and experience the rewards."

"Well, Ingrid, you don't look nearly as old as the wisdom you dispel." Unable to contain his amusement at her fortune-telling, he replied. "He'll be back on the 27th."

"Bernard! That's wonderful, I do miss him."

Then reality struck her. "What does that mean for you, Logan?"

"At this point, it's in Chef Marceau's hands. My hands are tied until I hear from him again."

"Then it must be that way, but my hands are not tied."

Ingrid winked and disappeared in a flash, finding Flaxie

waiting by the tree.

"I haven't been able to think of anything but our going home to the apartment. I've gone over every detail in my head."

"It will be whatever you want it to be. Take a deep breath. Shall we take the elevator then?"

Flaxie rambled in nervousness. "I haven't even gone to Uncle Bernard's apartments very often because of the . . . the obstacle." Her face suddenly lit up. "But I loved traveling in the elevator with my parents."

At the ding of the elevator doors reaching the penthouse floor, she froze momentarily, then took a breath of courage.

Ingrid led her to the double door and jangled a brass ring of keys. With a few tries, she found the correct one.

The latch held tight at first, then a comforting click released all the memories of seventeen years ago. Stepping across the threshold, she waved Flaxie to follow, then opened the curtains and turned on the lights.

Flaxie stepped inside the entry hall with the parlor straight ahead. There was the hearth where she remembered playing when the world stopped for her. Ahead was the staircase to the west turret where she'd spent childhood hours watching the dots moving up and down the slopes of Mont Blanc.

The stark silence was interrupted when Ingrid turned on the old record player. It was still pre-stacked as time had stopped the past. It crackled with the start of Bing Crosby, crooning 'I'll Be Home for Christmas'.

"Ouch, that song is painful," Flaxie said. She slumped back into her father's favorite armchair and hugged the cushion to her chest.

"Ingrid, after all these years I can detect the scent of Papa's aftershave as if he were still in this very room. I should have come sooner."

Ingrid set about removing dust sheets off the parlor furniture and straightened the family photos on the mantle.

"Why did Grandmama, Grandpa, and Uncle Bernard close the door and forget them?"

"They never forgot your parents, dear, it was too painful. Your uncle did his best to spare you pain. Don't fault him if you don't agree, he only wanted to protect you."

"I could never fault Uncle Bernard. However, he doesn't see that I have become a woman and not his little girl."

"He is facing that now and may have regrets but he always wanted what was best for you, Flaxie."

Ingrid reached out her hand. "Now come along, let's look in the tea cupboard and you can check out your mother's bureau."

"When I would have a tea party with Mama, she got out a wonderful cinnamon orange spice and her special china cups. My favorite had tiny pink roses and purple violets on four golden legs. Do you think there would be some in the cupboard?"

"I'll see what I can find."

Flaxie poked her head into the kitchen when the kettle whistled to find Ingrid washing her cherished cups.

"Look, Ingrid, this is Mama's Christmas cape with the hood and fur trim, still with a whiff of Channel No. 5. I tend to log scents with my memories. I find it comforting."

Reminiscing over her discoveries, Flaxie felt at home at last as she walked through her past resurrecting memories. Unwrapped Christmas presents were stacked in the corner of the living room. She squatted on the floor surrounded by boxes wrapped with colorful foils and bows.

"Look, Ingrid, my parents got me the talking doll I wanted when I was little . . . and a dancing Barbie and my favorite Donna Parker books. Unfortunately, these new dresses, sweaters, and black patent shoes won't fit me."

With a shoebox from the closet, she sat beside Ingrid on the sofa. "These are old love letters between my parents. Do you think they'd mind if I read them?"

"If anyone should, it is you, dear, but look how time as flown. Logan will expect us in the dining room now. We can come back soon, or if you wish, you could take the box with you."

"Yes, I'd like to take this one with me."

Her eyes fell on an envelope addressed to Francesca Stanhope before her marriage. The address was from a convent in Venice.

"Peculiar!"

16

Woodcutter's Cabin

Bernard's competitive challenge at the King George that evening would be a five-course menu under the discreet scrutiny of the most critical judges. He decided on the seared scallops, ginger spears with garlic lemon caper sauce. In anticipation, he rose before the sun and went off to the early seafood market in Marais.

His pursuit was satisfied, adding the day's catch for his creative bouillabaisse, then fresh lamb and venison for his veal stew, winter berries for a tiered cream napoleon with Pavlova, and exotic cheeses, dried fruits, edible herbs, and wildflowers.

"The Michelin inspectors have remained under the radar, however, I do suspect Monsieur Raymonde," he mused. "The man is skinny as a rail and only accepts a minuscule sample. For the life of me though, I cannot understand how a true connoisseur of food can tolerate those pencil mustaches. Surely it interferes with the aroma and taste of the food."

Tonight's dinner in the Vienna Salon would be evaluated by three judges and three chefs who had not yet been announced.

"Surely if Director Morningside were to be a judge, I would take Logan's advice with the Turbot à la Normande with shrimp, mussels, leeks, spinach, and champagne sauce."

A light mist of rain in the air inspired Marceau in expediting his excursion. Walking spritely on the boulevard, his mind was back at Mont Blanc anticipating Ingrid's welcome.

His mind raced to ponder over the tiniest of details.

"Perhaps I will ask Logan to have a fine romantic dinner catered in my apartment. And flowers, I must arrange for roses. Life will be very different, with so many changes in the New Year, and they will all good."

Swinging his umbrella in one hand, he pulled his grocery trolley as he sauntered back to the hotel. With no one in hearing range, he broke into spontaneous humming of 'Singing in the Rain'. Out loud, he laughed at himself, at the urge to kick up his feet like Gene Kelly, but was reminded of his girth.

Above Chamonix, the snow fell heavily. Flaxie checked with Dion about the influx of visitors crowding the cafés.

"Roberto, if this snow continues, we will have a wonderful white Christmas. After dinner tonight, our full rehearsal in the ballroom will go over the routines with live music. Check with the jesters, performers, and yodelers that they will come for the trial.

"Also, slot in a song sketch for Logan . . . I'll tell you more about that later. I hope the thick snow doesn't slow the cog

A Wenceslas Christmas 121

tram or the shuttle cats."

When Flaxie finally took a breath, Dion was looking at her with a smirk and his palm raised.

"My dear, Mademoiselle Marceau, everything will take its course. It's the season to relax and enjoy every moment. Sometimes unanticipated deviations are the most delightful."

An hour later, Hunter Bodine arrived to report that the warning flag was up, for the hotel to alert skiers to seek alternate activities.

Flaxie stepped outside in her parka and looked up toward the mountains. Bodine joined her.

"See way up there . . . the old woodcutter's cabin? Its roof is covered in snow. Are they safe?"

"Odd that you bring that up," he said. "Minutes ago their chimney smoke was expelling in erratic puffs. Normally, Alpine distress signals are six in a minute, then a pause and repeat. Would he know that or was it a coincidence? Either way . . ."

"Do any children live there?"

"Three little girls. I was there in the summer. The Missus is also expecting a Christmas baby. The house was stark, but they had the brightest smiles and begged me to stay for stew and dumplings."

Flaxie became jittery. "Hunter, if the puffs were meant as calls for help . . . with a new baby due now, wouldn't a midwife or doctor check on them, if they could get through?"

"Hunter said, "I don't have spare personnel, but I have a snowmobile, a rescue traverse, snowshoes, and a medical pack. Can you think of anyone that could be a substitute midwife, if needed? And they'll need food and blankets."

"We'll move fast," she said. "Come inside."

In the kitchen, Roberto was chatting with Marianne and

the staff about the rehearsal. Logan took off his apron for the impromptu meeting and Flaxie rushed to him.

"Hunter and I think the Chiasson chalet on the hill is sending an S.O.S. signal. Hunter will get together travel equipment as roads won't be passable with the truck. We'll need blankets, flashlights, fuel, and food. Madame Chaisson may be in labor. Has anyone delivered a baby, perhaps a nurse or midwife?"

Marianne cleared her throat. "Under the circumstances, I confess I have a nursing degree that I got straight out of university before I decided on cooking. I've assisted in a few births and I'll can certainly be of help."

Logan took immediate charge with the decisions. "Hunter, you guide the rescue party. Flaxie and I will join you. Marianne, you'll join the search and prepare to assist Madame Chaisson."

He paged Roberto Dion and found him right away. "The last of the dinner guests can be attended by Magnon and Collins. Monsieur Dion, you and Ingrid will be in charge of the rehearsal tonight."

In the flurry of activity, supplies were packed quickly. As Marianne collected medical supplies, Flaxie wrapped hot meals for the family and filled a hamper with baked goods and candies for the children.

"I have an idea," Marianne squealed. "On Christmas Eve, Father Christmas will give out gifts. Roberto and I wrapped puzzles, coloring books, dolls, and tinker toy cars. A few could be spared for the trip."

"Marianne, go ahead," Flaxie said. "For three little girls, and collect some linens, towels, and anything else for a newborn."

Flaxie took the elevator to the penthouse and returned with a laundry bag filled with the presents that her parents had left for her years before.

Minutes later, the foursome was ready, with a supply sled and traverse hitched and lashed on the backs of two snowmobiles. Hunter tested the walkie-talkies and gave one to Logan. Both were concerned as the snowfall was becoming heavier as they loaded.

"There won't be much of a trail, so trust my instincts and experience in the hills. It should take an hour to reach the summit by the cabin. Are you all ready?"

Logan revved up the engine. "Ready," he said. Flaxie, behind him, held her arms firmly around his waist and sang the words still in her mind.

Yonder peasant, who is he?
Where and what his dwelling?
Sire, he lives a good league hence,
Underneath the mountain,
Right against the forest fence
By Saint Agnes fountain.

At the sound of her voice, Logan squeezed her arm.

"It's a wonderful feeling I have today, to help a family in need. I'm pumped for this," Flaxie said, and the wind took her words as they sped from the hotel.

Within half an hour, the snowfall gusts were blinding their vision, slowing the rescue. Hunter radioed to forge ahead rather than to seek shelter and become trapped themselves.

In the darkness, Logan strained to keep the lights of Bodine's vehicle in view. The radio crackled and faded until they were unable to decipher Hunter's instructions, then nothing.

"I hear the roar of his engine not far ahead," Flaxie said.

"Can you see anything? The cabin must be close."

Through the blustering snow, a distant lantern was swinging. "Is it Hunter, or Monsieur Chaisson?"

A weak voice called through the wind. "Help! Help!"

Logan slowed the snowmobile until he could see the ranger's unit just ahead, but no one was on it.

"Help! Help! Over here."

Shutting down the engine, Logan held Flaxie's hand as they trudged toward the voice, then bumping straight into Marianne and Hunter.

In the filtered light, the silhouette of a man stood at the cabin door. "Come in quickly. I'm October Chaisson, but people call me Otto."

Otto was frail and about to collapse as he wept. "Mon Dieu! The baby is not coming right, I don't know what to do."

Hunter and Marianne followed the woodcutter inside where a woman was writhing on a bed. Across the room, three little girls huddled together beside a barely warm wood stove.

Marianne sprang into action demanding linens and hot water as she rushed to Madame Chaisson.

"Shh . . . we're here to help you, dear."

Marianne suddenly became the sainted nurse Evangeline as she stroked her head. "Be calm and relax your breathing and only push when I ask you. What is your first name, Madame Chaisson?"

"Merci, merci, please call me Jan, for January."

Marianne's smile and voice were comforting. "Jan, I have medical training as a nurse. You are about to deliver in the next few minutes. You are doing a fine job and your girls are so well behaved."

A Wenceslas Christmas

As Flaxie boiled water, Logan carried in more firewood and stoked up the stove. Hunter, in a red ranger parka, first brought in the supplies, then the mysterious sack of gifts.

Logan listened quietly to the three girls, discussing whether or not Hunter might be the real Father Christmas.

They were thin and undernourished and wore passed down clothing much too big, but Logan watched their wondrous blue eyes as they waited in anticipation of the movements about the room.

"It's impossible, April, Father Christmas doesn't know where we live, besides he's never found us before," the elder one said.

"June, he will *neve*r come if you don't believe in him."

May, the youngest, had a tearful plea. "I've been good all year, Mama even said so."

Logan slid over to sit by the girls. "In the springtime, do you remember seeing the big hotel down the hill? It's been there forever."

"Yes, it is like a castle," April said. "We watch on the hills during lambing season. Mama gives us special bottles for the newborns, and they watch us too."

As they spoke, Logan watched the peace on the three small faces waiting for words of hope and a promise of Christmas.

"We have come from the hotel. We saw your Papa's smoke signal and thought we could help. Father Christmas sends a helper to the hotel to greet guests on Christmas morning. He was preparing his sleigh when we were leaving and he sent a special sack for your cabin. He said to tell you he's sorry he cannot always get up the mountain."

"Oooh!" The smallest was fully enthralled as her eyes darted to the sacks by the door.

"Father Christmas sent you?"

"Yes, but now while your Ma is busy having a new baby, I can read you a Christmas story."

His eyes searched the room where there might be toys or books and found none.

"It's no matter, I can recite 'Twas the Night Before Christmas by heart. Would you like that?"

Their shy giggles said yes, and with awe, they hung onto every word, imagining visions of sugar plums, sleighs, and the jolly, red elf in the sky.

Flaxie kept back tears watching Logan's wisdom with the girls. The cabin was cozy now, but Marianne still had a concern.

"Flaxie, please time Madame's contractions. We will need her to push longer. The baby needs to come soon or he will have too much difficulty. It is taking too long."

Otto Chiasson overheard her. "Did you say 'he'?"

"I didn't mean to say that, Monsieur, we don't know yet. The best thing you can do is hold your wife's hand and soothe her. Tell her of your hopes and dreams and of the good times you've shared here on the mountain."

Dejection set on his face as he clasped her hand. "Jan, I'm sorry I haven't provided better. One day I promise you a new store-bought dress and a wool coat for winter. The baby will never want for love, or will you, my dearest."

Minutes later a feeble cry brought the room to silence. Marianne worked feverishly loosening a tightened birth cord, then patted the babe to a hearty cry.

"He is good but a bit small," Marianne whispered in relief. "Do you have a name for your son?"

Jan looked at her husband and swaddled the baby in her arms. "His name will be December."

The three others crowded around their mother to see the

tiny infant. "Oh, Mama, he looks just like me," June said.

As Marianne attended to January and the baby, the others warmed up a feast from the hampers. Out of sight, Logan filled stockings for the girls with toys, books, and treats as Flaxie taught the children to cut snowflake patterns for decorations.

A blast of snow sprayed through the doorway as Hunter stepped out for sprigs of evergreen to string up a garland over the hearth.

With hot dishes, evergreen décor, and candles, the family sat to feast. The four from the hotel said they had eaten and joined the family to chat through dinner.

The meager tales of the family's pride and survival on the mountain told them of avalanches, wolves, hunger, and loneliness. The contrast was painful to Flaxie and stirred her emotions.

By the door was a rack of coats including the visitors' parkas. Flaxie was drawn to a tattering one, of rags and bits of sheepskin.

"January, this sheepskin coat . . . is it yours? Could I try it on?"

"It's not much but it gets me through our winters."

Flaxie slipped her arms into the sleeves. "It's wonderful. I could never find one like it in the village."

She held out her red down jacket with the fur-lined hood. "Would you consider trading with me for my winter parka?"

"Oh, that is much too fine a coat for me."

"Please accept it as a Christmas present as I will mine."

Flaxie smoothed her hands over the tattered furrows. "I will always remember the Chiasson family each time I wear my new coat."

At the door, Hunter shook hands with the family, but it

was clear he was burdened. "I work with a Red Cross station at the village. When the storm clears, I'll return with a doctor to check on December. We brought supplies on a medics sleigh but the other is a sturdy toboggan, and I'll leave that here for you. I'll have peace of mind knowing you will be able to reach the hotel anytime. Is your dog team and sled in the shed?"

The emotional woodcutter was unable to speak but he hugged Hunter in gratitude for the many gifts of this day.

June tugged at Hunter's coat. "Gita, our old dog, died in a mudslide. Darnit just got really old and then poor little Gimpy . . ." she looked away sadly.

Hunter bent down, experiencing a new, unexpected level of humility. "June, when I return after the snow, I'll bring replacements and extra food supplies for your family and a new dog team too."

Little June was already on her toes and jumped over and over at the news. "Oh, that would be lovely. This is our best Christmas." The tiny girl hugged Hunter, then her mother and dad.

On the snowmobile, Flaxie whispered to Logan.
"Ye who now will bless the poor
Shall yourselves find blessing."
"What a meaningful day," he said. "I'm very thankful."
"Thank you for telling me about Good King Wenceslas. I am blessed from today and I loved sharing it with you. My heart is full. It was an inspiration I won't forget, also seeing the roles of Hunter and Marianne in this rescue, bringing a new life into the world."

As the gusts had weakened, they found their old path down and arrived back at the Grand Marceau minutes before midnight.

"So much easier downhill with the hotel in a spectacular blaze of light," Logan said. "It looked glorious from the mountain."

"Yes, glorious, that's what it is."

At the veranda, they shook their coats free of snow, then allowed Ernesto to take them in for care. He tilted his head and examined the tattered sheepskin.

"I see you've been a Good Samaritan!"

17

The Meaning of Christmas

Roberto and Ingrid were in armchairs by the great tree waiting for an accounting of the night. At their voices, Ingrid jumped to her feet.

"Come in here and warm up with us by the fireplace. Flaxie, you're shivering!"

She removed a knitted shawl from her shoulders. "Put this around you, I've warmed it up waiting."

Roberto snapped his fingers and a lad in waiter's garb jogged over for the order. "From the looks of the lot of you, a hot whiskey or a mulled wine is in order."

Marianne wriggled in a frenzy to tell their story. "Before you talk about the rehearsal, I'm bubbling over about our amazing adventure."

She leaned forward with her elbows on her knees, with Hunter propped on the arm of her chair. Ingrid's eyes glistened in anticipation.

"Hunter can explain how we arrived at the cabin, but I had the glorious privilege to deliver a newborn—it was a miracle."

Marianne crossed herself with prayer and raised her hands in thanksgiving.

"I was scared when we got there. January had been struggling and the baby's color wasn't good. Hunter said to force my fear aside and do what I had been trained while nursing. So I did that. When I asked for January's final push, he wiggled, then a faint cry and I knew it was a blessed birth."

In silence, they shared her emotion.

"The villages around Mont Blanc have always had a shortage of midwives," Hunter added.

"In what condition is the family?" Ingrid asked.

"Sparse living quarters," Flaxie said. "They needed any supplies you'd name. The girls didn't expect that Father Christmas knew where they lived, but Logan assured them we received Santa's message. Their eyes danced with belief and trust.

"We served them a meal and filled stockings by the fireplace. When we left, baby December had a healthy cry in his mother's arms. Thank you, Hunter, for leaving the toboggan and promising to return with a medic."

Her voice cracked. "And he is taking them a new dog sled team."

As Marianne watched Hunter with pride, Flaxie was struck how they had grown so much as a couple.

"Now about the rehearsal," Logan said as his adrenaline settled.

"Our story pales in comparison, but it was fun for all," Roberto said. "The actors arrived in plenty of time and the scripts had no flaws. The Father Christmas play kept us all in stitches including the performers, but if it hadn't been for Ingrid, my costume might have failed."

Ingrid said, "My only wish to make it perfect would have been for your Uncle Bernard to be here. There hasn't been this much joy at the Grand since the year I arrived. I am so proud to be part of this family."

Soon the gathering around the storytellers had grown to add curious guests and staff, with rounds of hot chocolate, beverages, and shortbreads.

Logan rose with a glass. "A toast to everyone! "A Merry Christmas to each of you. And to Good King Wenceslas for sending us up the mountain."

Roberto Dion started up a sing-a-long, and the party continued into the night with uproarious laughter and songs until it dawned on the managers to wind it down.

"Thank you for this memorable night," Logan said "We get swept up in the functions of the hotel, but Christmas should also be in our hearts and deeds.

"We're lucky to have warm homes with food and friends, but others in the village, especially at the hostel, are far from family. For them, Christmas can be meager and lonely.

"At the end of every generous meal, we have waste. But this year, after the Christmas Eve buffet, we'll box up hot meals and take packages to the hostel for those less fortunate. I'll coordinate the food but I'll need volunteers to deliver meals in the truck and take greetings."

Whether from mulled wine or Christmas spirit, the room buzzed again with voices and energy, with more than a dozen hands raised.

Hunter said, "If there are too many for the Vulcan, I can take my vehicle."

"I'll go with Hunter," Marianne said.

"God bless you every one. We'll meet in the ballroom at

eleven tomorrow night. Be prepared to bring our Christmas spirit into Chamonix!"

As they dispersed, Logan cornered Roberto.

"Tell me about Father Christmas. I heard complimentary reports of the unknown bearded gentleman."

"It was like a dream to me, reflecting on my earliest memory of climbing on the old man's knee. His magnificent beard had tickled me and the warmth of his smile convinced my suspicious heart.

"If one child's Christmas will be more thrilling from my portrayal of the real Father Christmas, I will have pleasure for a lifetime. It's the greatest experience."

The next day was Christmas Eve, and from the earliest morning hours, the bustle consumed the staff. Hotel events were foremost on Flaxie's mind, and Logan was focused on preparing the traditional feast.

In Chamonix, the last train pulled into Place de la Gare depot filled to half capacity. Passengers emptied onto the platform to wait for the luggage compartment to be opened.

A haggard, curly, blond-haired lad, with a canvas rucksack and a leather portfolio under his arm, disembarked and headed directly for the hostel at the end of Main Street.

18

A Joyful Feast

A wind ensemble of a flute, bassoon, and clarinet sat in a circle stage by the Christmas tree playing 'Joy to the World' as patrons awaited the show.

Flaxie, Ingrid, and Roberto stood at the ballroom door with personal greetings as guests entered. From the week's hype of the mysterious show, over-excited children giggled and danced in anticipation.

Ernesto waited in the entry assisting old Mrs. Thompson in her wheelchair through the line. Sighting Flaxie, the lady suddenly waved her hand. "Please stop here, Ernesto."

He wheeled her to Flaxie at the door. "My dear girl, thank you for the flowers you sent this week. They are exactly what my Nathaniel would have ordered for me. It was so kind of you to remember." Mrs. Thompson's hand clasped Flaxie's.

She whispered a thank you to Ernesto for forwarding Hunter's unwanted flowers, then winked across at Ingrid.

A Wenceslas Christmas 135

As the ballroom filled, the outer doors closed and as the lights turned down, the stage spotlights went up.

Instantly the atmosphere broke into a fast-paced frivolity with a musical prelude by an oompah band with its spontaneous clapping and toe-tapping.

Juliette, in a glittering sequin red cinnamon dress, took center stage as master of ceremony and welcomed guests and volunteers to the festivities.

"Our skits begin with a story of Pepita, a poor girl who wants to honor the birth of Jesus but cannot afford a votive candle at her church to offer a Christmas Eve prayer. Pepita is played by a hotel guest, Delia Forrester, and her brother Pedro by Hans Brockmeier. The music is from the village woodwind ensemble that serenaded you in the lobby.

"Then we'll go directly to a marionette play visiting the elves' hectic workshop on Christmas Eve, featuring the Chamonix player's group. Special thanks to the alpine minstrels who taught alpine yodeling and dance traditions to many of your children this week."

In the wings, Roberto Dion paced quietly, concentrating on his entrance.

"Our feature play begins now with Father Christmas preparing for Christmas Eve after a dream. In a visit to the busy market, he encounters townsfolk and characters that remind him of the meaning of the season. You will see the hustle and bustle of shoppers in their last-minute shopping."

Juliette curtsied as the curtain raised to find Father Christmas rising from his night's sleep.

To the cheers from the crowd, Dion rubbed the sleep from his eyes and stretched and strolled to the stage in elaborate layers of cloaks, polished boots, and a furry crown decked with holly berries. After a comedy routine of morning chores and preparations, he reviewed his fabled list so he could finalize his shopping.

"Ho, Ho, Ho. So many good boys and girls are on the Naughty and Nice list, and a number of them are right here at the Grand Marceau. Let me check it once more . . ."

Applause and children's laughter encouraged a cast of dancing and cartwheeling elves onto the stage, creating mayhem for Father Christmas. Actors as shoppers paraded next with complaints or inspirations.

Finally, a blow-up discussion was resolved by Father Christmas, reminding villagers that the spirit of Christmas comes from the heart and can't be bought in the store or found under the tree.

The cheering from children and parents drowned out Roberto Dion as he started at the microphone, then hushed in anticipation of words from Father Christmas.

"I have a true story, boys and girls, moms and dads—it happened right here on Mont Blanc. With the magnificent mountains behind us, we have the luxury to sleep in fine hotels and enjoy gourmet food. However, it's not like this for everyone.

"The other day, Ranger Bodine saw an S.O.S. signal up on the mountain from an isolated chalet. A woodcutter and his family of three little girls live there. The avalanche had cut off their access and they were cold, hungry, and lonely, and their mother lay in labor.

"But they didn't lack for love for each other and they had never complained about the things they didn't have.

"In the blinding snow, Ranger Bodine led Chef Powell, Flaxie Marceau, and our assistant sous-chef Marianne up the mountain with two sleds, with food, supplies, fuel, a medical bag, and a Santa sack. When they arrived, the woodcutter's wife was having a difficult birth, and thankfully Marianne helped.

A Wenceslas Christmas

"A fire was stoked and a Christmas feast prepared, with stories read to the children. Stockings were filled by the hearth, with a promise to return with supplies and more companionship, everything the family could have wanted."

The room was silent in awe, wanting to hear more.

"Chef Powell has a story, near to his heart, of the old traditional carol from King Wenceslas of Prague. Listen to the lyrics of the tale of the kindly king sharing goodwill with the woodcutter." Dion gestured for Logan and Flaxie.

"Christmas is a time to think of others less fortunate," Logan said. "True, it was an honor to be part of Christmas at the woodcutter's house, however, that is not enough.

"After tomorrow's Christmas Eve buffet, we are taking boxed meals into Chamonix to those who can't be at home. We'll stop at the hostel and train station where travelers may be stranded, and find those unable to feast this Christmas. If you want to be part of that, we will leave from the foyer at 11 p.m. Now join in the words about this good king. Song sheets are on the chairs."

He pulled Flaxie closer. As they began, others stood to join, with voices filling the ballroom with the ancient carol.

Good King Wenceslas looked out
On the feast of Stephen,
When the snow lay round about,
Deep and crisp and even
Brightly shone the moon that night,
Though the frost was cruel,
When a poor man came in sight,
Gathering winter fuel.

Hither, page, and stand by me.
If thou know it telling,
Yonder peasant, who is he?

Where and what his dwelling?
Sire, he lives a good league hence,
Underneath the mountain,
Right against the forest fence
By Saint Agnes fountain.

Bring me flesh, and bring me wine.
Bring me pine logs hither.
Thou and I will see him dine
When we bear the thither.
Page and monarch, forth they went,
Forth they went together
Through the rude wind's wild lament
And the bitter weather.

In his master's step he trod,
Where the snow lay dented.
Heat was in the very sod
Which the saint had printed.
Therefore, Christian men, be sure,
Wealth or rank possessing,
Ye who now will bless the poor
Shall yourselves find blessing.

By the last words, the room was swaying, a makeshift choir of two hundred melodic voices singing of the mountain rescue by the kindly king and his page.

On the verge of panic, Roberto found Flaxie in the kitchen. His cheeks were flushed and his words erratic.

"We never expected what's happened now! I know you plan to deliver the meals to Chamonix by the shuttle and the ranger's truck. But more than half the audience insists on joining the delivery! We're not prepared to handle that many."

"Call in the transfer snow cats and ask for volunteer wagons. And send word to Chamonix—folks there will want to help when they find out. The charitable fever is so exhilarating, Roberto. We'll just make more food."

Her infectious giggles grew and started up his laughter too, then Logan overheard them and then Ingrid.

"We already have dozens of guests for this mission and more keep coming," Ingrid said.

Stunned by the reality, Logan's face eased to gratification. "Thank goodness I have you, Ingrid. I suppose if I could get the sleigh and the Clydesdales up on the roof, I'd be off at midnight."

Flaxie's heart swelled with love for this humble man in her life.

"I'm so proud of you, Logan."

The food platters at the réveillon buffet at the Grand Marceau overflowed beyond the normal on Christmas Eve.

The oyster bar was surrounded with scallops in foie gras sauce and prawns, and poached salmon with crème fraîche on crostini. Beside it was a roasted goose, then a crispy golden turkey or la dinde de Noël stuffed with chestnut sausage dressing and a juicy loin of apple-stuffed wild boar. Rows of gilt-edged tureens were filled with duchess potatoes, braised red cabbage, buttered root vegetables, sweet potato casserole drizzled with maple syrup, Brussel sprouts, cranberry orange chutney, and an array of sweet buns and miniature loaves of bread.

In the French tradition, the 'Thirteen Desserts' first acknowledged in Provence were displayed by Juliette, with buche de nöel log and warm baba au rhum, crêpes suzette, gingerbread cake with lemon sauce, cinnamon apple strudel, chocolate cream mousse, crème de caramel, wild blueberry pie, Dutch chocolate mirror cake, heavenly cherry cheesecake, tri-colored napoleons, macarons, and pavlovas.

Collins and the dining staff had worked through the day freshening the décor with garlands, polished candelabra, pots of crimson poinsettias, and linen napkins folded in reindeer shapes.

Chef Powell made his final review as guests' voices echoed outside the dining room doors.

Logan raised his hand to give his consent. "Magnificent! Let's open the doors."

19

Taking Goodwill to Chamonix

The lobby was bursting with late-night guests enjoying loud chatter as they waited for the Wenceslas pilgrimage.

On the incline to the hotel's portico, Hunter and Ernesto directed traffic for the excited volunteers to climb aboard. A spontaneous burst of 'Here Comes Santa Claus' started up on the first wagon and spread in a fevered pitch across to the entrance.

The kitchen assembly line bustled to pack meals and plastic cutlery in containers, Ingrid added stocking stuffers, and volunteers tied bright bows.

At the bay, Magnon and Collins teamed up to start loading the truck, and Logan updated the manifest for the village hostel, the train depot, and St. Mark's church in the town's center.

Flaxie wrapped her arms around Logan's waist.

"You know you have started an annual tradition on Mont Blanc."

But she could see he was suffering from conflict.

"You don't know how badly I'd like to say that you are right . . . but whether I'll be here next year is out of my hands. I phoned Paris and I'm waiting to hear from your uncle. He is facing a demanding challenge there and I don't want to cause him undue concern. But, yes, I have broached the idea of staying on.

"I think of nothing else every minute. You've become my heart and home. It's a dream come true, but the reality is not yet on my side as your uncle will return the day after tomorrow and I am still slotted back at the George a few days later."

Struck by his sentiment, Flaxie held both his hands. "You can't let that happen, I can't lose you. Logan, I love you. I've never said that to anyone since my parents died. Not even Uncle Bernard."

For Logan, the aching was painful. He looked across the room, knowing that staff in the working area was observing his quiet conversation with Flaxie. He wanted to take her in his arms and assure her everything would be alright but instead, he said the unthinkable.

"Can we talk about this later?"

"Later? Did you hear what I said, Logan?"

"Come with me." He directed her to a private corner.

"Please, Flaxie, just two more days. I wanted to deal with this man-to-man with your uncle but your enthusiasm has made that impossible. I love that about you and I do love you . . ."

Flaxie's finger touched his lips in mid-sentence.

"That's all that I needed, Logan . . . I was so afraid that you didn't love me the same as I love you."

A Wenceslas Christmas

She looked around, then blurted. "For heaven's sake, there must be some mistletoe around here somewhere."

Logan snatched a sprig of parsley from the counter and held it high, to the kitchen's applause. In the next moment, he felt more complete and alive as he held Flaxie in a tight embrace.

With a pirouette of her hand in the air, Ingrid gestured to the staff to resume their packing and shoved Logan and Flaxie into the chef's office.

"Talk this out, you two. Magnon, Collins, Juliette, Marianne, Roberto, and the others will take care of packages. Take a few minutes, then come out ready to get on with the deliveries . . . but savor this moment."

Flaxie followed Logan then flashed a grin of appreciation to Ingrid.

Hearing about Logan's conversation with her uncle, she shared a sigh of relief. "I'm sorry for my pressure. Now that I understand, I'll be patient. The important thing is that I love you. I want you to be in my life, however you decide that will be."

"For now, we'll complete the Wenceslas mission and cherish this Christmas spirit. We'll put our faith in your uncle's hands and face our future together."

"There's something else you need to know, Logan. Uncle Bernard isn't aware, but I came across documents a few years back about my inheritance. When I turn twenty-five in a few weeks, I will receive a hefty trust. Did you know about that?"

Logan couldn't deny the truth.

"Your Uncle mentioned that too, that if it didn't scare me then I was wrong for you. However, if it did frighten me, then I should fight for you. He said I would be able to make the right decision once I hear the story of your parents' romance. But I don't need to know their story, I have mine here with you."

With a kiss, she took his hand and led him out.

"The town awaits the Feast of Stephen."

Hunter and Marianne were waiting at the loading dock with supplies.

"Ernesto sent the groups ahead, to wait for your arrival," Hunter said. "Both vehicles are packed to the gills. Word is out around Chamonix and you might be surprised at the turnout. This is a good thing for all of Mont Blanc."

Marianne gave a butchy punch to the chef.

"Logan and I have worked as a team for several years, and I couldn't be more proud of him than today."

Logan's eyes connected with them both. "Marianne, don't forget the hero at the woodcutter's cabin. I hope you gave him proper congratulations."

Marianne squirmed. "Don't you worry, I showed him my appreciation."

As the convoy reached the village, louder cheering and applause roared through the streets that had built up for a spontaneous celebration.

Hunter and Marianne and a group of volunteers spread out through the crowd to give out meals to travelers sleeping in the train depot.

"I've never shared so much joy," Flaxie said. "Where have you been, Logan? In all the years with Christmas at the Grand, we never thought to have such an outreach, with the guests too."

Logan pointed at the wide-eyed residents that had emerged and now stood in front of the hostel.

"Humility, darling, this is for them."

A Wenceslas Christmas

At the back was a young lad with blond, curly hair, paralyzed with emotion. He didn't step forward with the others for a meal or gift pack but he intently watched Flaxie's every movement. His heart pounded with a new yearning to belong.

The hostel manager worked his way to Logan and Flaxie.

"It's an honor, folks. In the village, we heard legendary stories about Father Christmas going to the woodcutter's cabin. Then rumors of the Wenceslas Christmas have taken hold of everyone here.

"It's easy for folks down and out on their luck to be cynical at this time of year. We can't tell you how much this means. Many lonely young folks are here in the hostel and I know of one family with children waiting."

Ainsley Stanhope blended into obscurity, leaving him with disappointment and immediate regret at not initiating a meeting with his sister.

In Paris, Marceau picked up a packet of photographs from the local studio.

"I'm curious to see if the lad resembles Francesca."

Opening the envelope, he smiled. "Indeed, he does. I'll need to prepare Flaxie."

20

The Contestant, Chef Marceau

At the King George, Bernard Marceau was fine-tuning his finale recipe for Christmas Day. Every day, one of his competitors had been eliminated and the competition was more intense. Two days before Christmas, instructions were delivered to the final three, requiring their itemized ingredient lists.

Each contestant was assigned a cooling locker and a dedicated sous-chef. Bernard was relieved that he was conversant in Italian to communicate with Paulo, his underling, whose French was less than literate.

Over his kitchen pans, Bernard labored, refining, tasting, and seasoning until he reached perfection in his chicken black truffle consommé julienne.

Retrieving a thin crust of delicate puff pastry, he filled the nest with seared scallop and oyster tartare and prepared curried lemon cream for the second course.

Confident of the unique characteristics of his program, he began to detect and observe an air of jealousy by the hotel's resident staff.

His suspicion proved right when one of the prep chefs substituted Bernard's coarse salt with an inferior quality while he was retrieving other seasonings. In the distance, he caught not only the exchange but the guilty prep gloating to Augustus.

Chef Augustus of the King George was not a tall man without his chef's hat. He was clean-shaven and had a distinct round-shaped head, requiring the hat to be oversized over his shear crew cut.

Returning to his pans, Bernard knocked over the salt dish and replaced it himself to the chagrin of the culprit.

Predicting the need for security, he had brought the black truffle he'd acquired from Louis at Mont Blanc. Having paid dearly, he kept his specialties in his apron pockets to avoid confusion or mischief.

As he prepped a tureen of lobster foie gras sauce with a special seasoning from the fish market, Marceau observed Augustus' increasing scrutiny, contrary to competition rules that spices, techniques, and supplementary ingredients would be secret, revealed only when prizes were awarded.

He was uncomfortable with Augustus breathing down his neck and bristled as he caught glimpses of the resident chef prying into his black book notes and secrets.

It's ludicrous that a first-class chef by invitation cannot rely on his assigned kitchen support. Surely Director Morningside would not approve.

Was this a plan to get Logan out of the hotel and steal my creations? They cannot think this is a way to achieve another Michelin star. That would be utterly preposterous! I came to compete fairly, however, I gave Logan sage advice to grin and bear it so I must eat my words.

Marceau's Brest boned chicken was stuffed with slivers of black truffle pressed beneath the skin, then aged overnight in his cooler to absorb the true flavor.

With simmering chicken broth, truffle juice, port Madeira, and an aged Armagnac, he poached the poultry to tenderness in its succulent rich glaze. Baby croquettes of sweet onion-glazed new potatoes dotted the outer rim, surrounding the chicken on a bed of puréed cauliflower and spears of baby asparagus.

Marceau was aware of a whispered tête-à-tête between Augustus and the prep sous, then to runner delivering ingredients to the contestants.

Only three remained for the finale—Augustus, Marceau, and a Swiss chef Pierre Lafrondière. The Swiss chef also observed disruption to the salt dish from his workspace across the kitchen.

"Quite irregular!" Pierre declared. Peering over his eyeglasses, he saw a discreet opportunity to confide in Bernard, as Augustus was engrossed in preparing a shrimp mousse.

He sauntered to Bernard and quizzically broached it in a quiet aside. "The gastronomic organization surely would not risk its impeccable reputation. The hosts are more than generous, but I'm ashamed that I have questioned more than one presentation. Yesterday, Chef Blouin confided that his hollandaise sauce had been tampered with. Then today my whitefish was tainted. We must be more vigilant."

Bernard astutely withheld the secret of Augustus' past theft of Logan's cuttlefish recipe, to protect Powell's integrity.

"Yes, Chef Lafrondière, I agree we must guard our reputations wisely. I wish you much success in the finale tasting."

Marceau offered him a congenial handshake. "The week has been pleasant yet difficult, and I'm eager to return home, where my true prize awaits."

Director Morningside strutted into the culinary prep room and announced in a military voice that only one hour remained before the presentation.

Clicking a timing watch as if he fired the warning pistol, he turned with his head high and without pleasantries and returned to his sanctuary.

Bernard whispered to his helper, "Well, Paulo this is it! Ensure the plates are warmed precisely and fetch the accoutrements for presentation. I'll need a fresh sprig of rosemary and a few capers. Merci beaucoup."

Paulo winked. "Monsieur, my French is quite fine. I just pretended that I didn't understand when Chef Augustus asked me to spy on you—it gives me an advantage. I thoroughly enjoy a good game of chess."

Three international judges and two Michelin representatives waited in the Versailles Room for the covered tureens.

The three competitors were seated at a viewing table as each of the five courses was served. Samplings continued over the next half hour, then allowed fifteen minutes of deliberation.

Finally, an envelope was passed to Morningside declaring the decision for first, second, and third. The room fell silent awaiting his announcement.

Marceau watched the director's face as he opened the envelope. Stunned and confused, Morningside's eyes darted to judge No. 2, then to Chef Augustus.

Struggling to gain his composure, the rattled Morningside

stepped to the podium.

With minimal zeal, he dispatched the formalities.

"Before I introduce the winner, I must thank those that participated in all aspects, coming from many locations across Europe. We have been tantalized by the best cuisine this week. The ultimate decision of the judges awards the third place to the esteemed Chef Pierre Lafrondière of Geneva, Switzerland."

Assuming he was the winner and bathed in smugness, Augustus straightened himself to prepare for an acceptance speech. Then his eyes met Morningside's and his face went ashen.

"The winning results were very close between our own Chef Augustus and Chef Marceau . . . however, the inventive truffle and Madeira sauce on Marceau's Brest chicken was the favorite of all three judges. It is my honor to introduce the winner of the competition, Chef Bernard Marceau of Mont Blanc."

Ignoring the frowns of Augustus, Marceau was humble in his acceptance and patient with the magazine interviews, even offering his recipes for publication and touting his alpine establishment.

Returning to the culinary area to pack up his equipment and spices, he couldn't avoid the path of Augustus.

"Congratulations, Chef Marceau, but I am confused as to how your Madeira was not sour, it should have curdled the sauce."

"My dear Chef Augustus, you should strive for excellence on your own merit. That is much more satisfying than to use deceit or to borrow something that does not belong to you."

Augustus reddened, ready to dispute his interference.

"I will not argue with you, Augustus, or say anything

A Wenceslas Christmas

publicly. But I will have a chat with Director Morningside as he deserves the truth. This hotel needs a master chef and you have it in yourself to be that. However, I refuse to return your sous-chef. He deserves a better opportunity. Did you see Chouinard's critique?"

"I never should have permitted this in the beginning . . . if you had not come, everything would be as it should and Damien Chouinard would never have gone to Chamonix."

Bernard was aghast. "You dare to admit that you encouraged Monsieur Chouinard to take advantage of a chef's absence to defame his reputation?"

"Sometimes achievements come at a great expense and I am a better man for taking risks. I have risen in the ranks by my expertise and creativity. If you are jealous of me say so, but I should have won this competition."

"Regrets will do you no good. I'll give you half an hour to confess to hotel management before my departure interview with Morningside."

Augustus turned his back to walk away.

"Adieu Augustus! I don't think I need to bring to your attention that there are witnesses. I propose that you plead for probation to prove your worth."

21

The Proposal

Christmas Day at the hotel was festive and the brunch plans were in order. Flaxie decided that Roberto could be spared to spend the day with his family as Collins stepped up as an eager substitute in Customer Service.

Passing the front desk, Flaxie answered the manager's line. "Bonjour, Bon Noël, Merry Christmas."

"Flaxie, my dear, don't you know your uncle?"

"Uncle Bernard, we have missed you terribly. When are you coming home?"

"I've been trying to ring through to Ingrid, then Logan. But I get those dang answering machines. I have so much to tell you, Flaxie, and can't wait to see you. I don't have time now for a chat, but I need someone to pick me up at the train depot in Chamonix at 8:30 tonight."

"Certainly, Uncle, but don't they return the prize-winning chef in the same style as they took him . . . in a limousine?"

A Wenceslas Christmas

Bernard roared in laughter.

"My popularity seems to have waned. I'll tell you about that when I get home. I have to get going if I'm going to keep my connection. Merry Christmas, darling. One more thing, keep my return a secret from Ingrid, I'd like it to be a surprise. And tell Logan that I've worked it out."

Before she could ask him to elaborate, he had rung off. With her hand to her heart, she closed her eyes and smiled. "I knew Uncle Bernard could make everything right."

She was exuberant as she danced toward Logan's office with the good news. Marianne was on the sofa laughing in conversation with Logan.

She stopped at the door. "Sorry if I'm interrupting."

"Come in, Flaxie. I thought I should tell Logan first but you should know as well. I've discovered that, while I've been away from Paris, Jean-Paul has been two-timing me. But don't feel sorry for me, it's a relief. The night at the woodcutter's cabin changed my life. I found my soulmate and was reminded that I love helping people.

"Of course, my passion is cooking, but I've taken on part-time work as a mid-wife in Argentière. That way I can stay closer to Hunter. I won't be going back to Paris as this is where I want to be."

She jumped up and hugged Flaxie as she prepared to leave. "I hope you will be glad for me and Hunter too."

"Marianne, I'm indeed overjoyed. It's a wonderful day."

Logan sensed that Flaxie was bursting with news of her own, but she waited until Marianne was gone.

"Do you have a minute?"

"Always for you, Flaxie. Your face is glowing."

"Shh, a secret. I talked to Uncle Bernard and he is on his way home. He was in a hurry for the train but said to tell you he has worked it out. Oh, and Ingrid isn't to know when he's coming as he wants to surprise her."

"What about the competition? Did he win?"

"My gosh, I didn't even ask as I was so glad he's on his way."

"I'll find out right away."

He picked up the phone and dialed a valet's direct line at the King George. Hearing of the finale, he gave a thumbs-up to Flaxie.

"Thank you, Mario. I'll see you before too long. Have a Merry Christmas. What's that? A message for Chef Marceau that he must call Ainsley Stanhope? I'll tell him, I'm sure he knows what it's about."

Marceau sat in his first-class seat of the French National Railway car watching the scenery pass in a blur. He would change trains at Albertville then continue on a luxury motor coach in a long and inconvenient journey.

Over in his mind, he was finding the words he planned to say to Ingrid when he crossed the threshold of the Grand Marceau. For the nth time, he took the Tiffany box from his pocket and memorized every cut and sparkle of the diamond setting.

"I regret that Frederick is not here to stand with me, he would have wished us both well," he mused.

"I've been a fool not to have made this incredible realization when I was a younger man. I know Ingrid so well, yet I know so little about her past and her family, and I feel ashamed. I did promise Ingrid a dance at the New Year's gala and I'll not let her down or waste another year as a bachelor.

"There will be a lot of catching up in the next few days. My experience in Paris was not all that I had hoped for but it allowed me to reflect and seek conclusions. Willoughby is on track for the transition."

His face brightened as he mulled it over.

"Perhaps there will be more than one wedding soon, a birthday celebration for Flaxie in a few weeks, and hopefully a fruitful partnership with Logan Powell to ease my workload. And then there's Ainsley Stanhope."

The second seating of Christmas dinner had begun when Flaxie checked her watch.

"Sorry, Logan, but I must be off to the depot. I'll take the Vulcan if you don't object and I'll be back within the hour. It might be suitable to have a romantic table reserved by the fireplace. Don't let Ingrid miss me."

She raised herself on her toes to kiss him and snuck out the back.

"At least wear Marianne's coat and not the sheepskin," Logan called as an afterthought.

The Albertville coach was on schedule. As it pulled into the terminal at Chamonix, Bernard scanned the platform from the window, and Flaxie watched for him with anxious butterflies. With his valise in hand, Marceau heaved himself down the steps and into the arms of his niece.

"Merry Christmas. It is better than ever to see you, Flaxie," he whispered in her ear, refusing to release his embrace. "I'm glad I made it in time for a little celebration."

"It seems like ages as so much has happened."

"Indeed, my dearest, more than you know."

"Uncle Bernard, would you like to talk over a drink before we go to the hotel?"

"Normally yes, but I have an urgent matter on my heart and I need to go home. We'll talk as you drive."

He couldn't resist taking the jeweler's box from his pocket. "Do you think she'll like it?"

"Ingrid will be ecstatic, Uncle. She doesn't know you're here. Roberto took the day off to be with his family so she is hosting in the dining room. I asked Logan to reserve a romantic table by the fireplace." Flaxie giggled. "This is the best Christmas ever. We have so many stories and dreams to share."

"The table is an excellent thought. We Marceau's think alike." He laughed at the thought. "Now where can I get last-minute roses?"

"I'll get in touch with the ranger. He has become sweet on Logan's assistant, Marianne. No doubt he'll come to the hotel when she is finished her shift. He can fetch roses in the village."

"Hunter? My goodness, things have changed indeed."

Bernard was nervous that everything must be exact. "Let's not make a big front door arrival so I can surprise Ingrid. Park the truck in the rear."

"I'll distract her in the dining room as you get to the elevator with your bags. Don't worry, I won't let her escape."

Minutes later, the comical vision of the large bearded man slinking across to the elevator bay, incognito in his hotel, was noticed only by Collins.

"Flaxie, was that your uncle just now? I didn't think he was due back until tomorrow."

She winked. "You didn't see anything, Collins."

Ingrid was wearing a shamrock green cocktail dress with a Christmas corsage of white holly berries. Her hair was swept up into a bouffant with pearl and rhinestone combs and fine drop pearl earrings. Returning her claret red hostess jacket to the staff room, she encountered Flaxie in the main lobby.

"We've been so busy these days, I'm afraid I've forgotten

A Wenceslas Christmas

to eat. Flaxie, do you fancy joining me for a late dinner?"

"The best table is over by the fireplace. It says reserved, but the couple didn't show. Settle there and I'll find us some champagne."

"I won't make any objections. My feet are swollen from standing all day and rushing around. I have a new appreciation for Collins."

"The good news, Ingrid, is that the peak of our rush is over and we can ease into a slower pace."

Behind the pair, the great Marceau eased his chef's bulk into the dining room, dressed in a fine black suit, crisp white shirt, and charcoal and burgundy striped tie.

His eyes watered with emotion as he stopped meters away with a bouquet of red roses in the crook of his arm.

Ingrid was the first to see him.

"My goodness, Bernard, why didn't you tell me you were coming? I would have been at the door to greet you."

She rose from her chair, confused about his immediate intention.

"No, Ingrid, it is my turn to fuss over you. I wanted this to be a surprise. I've traveled all day to get here to be with you for Christmas dinner."

He nodded to the champagne bucket, but Ingrid was astounded as she tried to comprehend what was happening, seeing Bernard like a dazzled prom date holding out the bouquet.

Flaxie kissed each of them on the cheek then scurried away to find Logan and watch from the kitchen porthole.

Gently, Marceau held Ingrid in his arms and she sank her head against his shoulder.

"Ingrid, my dearest, I've imagined this moment since I

left for Paris in the limousine. I knew right away that my heart was being torn by the separation from the love of my life."

Spellbound from the unexpected fairytale romance that was unfolding, she hadn't spoken a word. With his hand touching her face, he kissed her until they both cried and laughed together.

"I've missed you too, Bernard. Since I arrived on your doorstep I longed for this day. I would wait another twenty years but I'm glad I won't have to. No one else makes my heart beat as you do."

Her eyes studied the features of his face as she stroked his cheek softly. "I know every inch in my sleep."

"The day I was leaving, I promised you a dance at the gala, but I want more than that."

He struggled to lower to one knee. "Ingrid Straussman, you are my soulmate, the love of my life, my heart, my soul, my future . . . will you marry me?"

"Yes, yes, yes!"

Righting himself, he sagged back into the chair. "It's time for a champagne toast to celebrate this moment, my darling." In an instant, the sommelier arrived.

Barely aware in the whirlwind, Ingrid blushed like a schoolgirl. "Bernard, you must have had an accomplice in these romantic arrangements."

He roared with laughter. "Eric, tell the curious young lady peering through the porthole that it's okay to come out."

Without prompting, Flaxie rushed through the swinging door to their table. Ingrid stood for her embrace, then held out her dazzling ring.

"It is not easy to trick me. You two were very clever and I'm overwhelmed and grateful."

"Well, you are truly two peas in a pod," Flaxie gushed.

"You're meant for each other and I'm thrilled for both of you."

"I've had time for serious thought while I was away," Bernard said. "As I'm not getting younger, can we put together a humble but extraordinary wedding for New Year's Eve? I see no need for a long engagement."

Ingrid was flushed with elation. "Oh yes, it can be a simple ceremony with family and friends. What about the panorama sunroom? Then we could join the ballroom party. Flaxie, you'll stand with me?"

"Of course, that's where I belong."

Bernard had already thought of details in his organized ways. "I thought I would ask Roberto to be my best man, and I was wondering, Ingrid, if you have folks in Austria that should come."

It was the first time Flaxie saw a hint of sadness in Ingrid's face. "The Marceaus are my family. I was eighteen when I came here twenty years ago. I'm embarrassed to say that I have no family. I spent my childhood in convents and orphanages and there are no brothers, sisters, or cousins to look for."

"Ingrid, I wish I had known to help you with your pain," Bernard said. "You've given so much happiness to this family. I've been selfish never to have asked about your past."

"Days gone by can't be changed, but I don't want to labor for even a moment on sadness when I have so much happiness now, Bernard."

Magnon stood by with a silver tray of appetizers.

"What have you brought us? We haven't even ordered."

"Chef Logan created a special menu for you. The first course is the sampling enjoyed by the gourmet critic,

Monsieur Chouinard. It's only right that you have a taste yourself."

Bernard tucked his thumbs behind his suspenders. "Let's enjoy this attention, Ingrid," he tooted. "Fine company and fine food."

"In the finest establishment," she said.

After the first course, Bernard waved for the server. "Is it possible to meet your chef, I'd like to give him my compliments for the succulent taste and this superb presentation?"

Logan arrived with a smirk as Bernard rose. "Chef Powell, I've heard interesting things about you in the past days. Damien Chouinard's article raised many eyebrows in Paris. From the tastes tonight, I would agree with him that the flavors are an exceptional and unexpected delight to the taste buds.

"I suggest a conference with you in the morning. Tonight I am focused on my beautiful fiancé, planning our future."

"Of course. My congratulations to both of you. I confess, Monsieur Marceau, that I borrowed your shadow while you are away."

"Ah, you refer to my lovely Ingrid."

"Bernard, I don't wish to intrude on your private and personal matters, however, I should tell you I took Flaxie to her parents' apartment. I'm not sure why I was apprehensive in waiting so long to push for that, but she was thrilled.

"Have you thought about our living arrangements? If we reside in your penthouse apartment, you could consider making Frederick's apartment available to Flaxie? It would keep the family close. I believe she is ready to return."

"It's a wise thought, Ingrid. I met with Willoughby in Paris. Time has passed quickly, and on her birthday in a few weeks, she will have access to her full trust account. I'm unprepared for what she may want to do with her future but I know that Logan Powell has become an integral part. I'll need your woman's instinct to guide me through these decisions."

"I have always guided you with my instincts. Life does not turn upside down when we get married, Bernard, it only gets better. We'll go forward as a united front."

"See . . . this is exactly the sort of thing I missed, being apart from you. It was like losing my left foot," he teased.

As the last of the dining patrons had departed, the two were alone by the fire. He motioned to Juliette, who was on the way with a carafe of coffee.

"Juliette, the dessert was wonderful. I see that you are closing up and I hope we haven't kept you. I wish you and your family a Merry Christmas. Are Logan and Flaxie still about?"

22

Flaxie's Inheritance

Logan was still in the kitchen—he had so much to tell Marceau. He didn't know where to begin and couldn't deter from his romantic celebration with Ingrid.

"You're still up, Logan," Juliette said. "Chef Marceau asked to speak with you again."

Marianne was waiting for Hunter and enjoyed watching Logan twist in his hesitation. "Tell him about the woodcutter and the Wenceslas expedition, he will hear about it soon enough."

"Thanks, Marianne. I'm learning to heed a woman's advice."

"Sit down Logan, we need to talk."

Ingrid said, "Shall I give the two of you privacy?"

"No, Ingrid, it's not necessary. We are now one heart and I will hold no secrets from you."

"I have many questions," Logan said. "But first I should update you on some events on Mont Blanc while you were gone."

Bernard was spellbound at the heroics of the mountain rescue to the woodcutter's house and was emotionally moved by the pauper family in distress.

"I give credit to Hunter Bodine, Marianne, and Flaxie for the miracle of life and bringing Christmas to the forgotten."

Logan took pleasure at the children's names, April, June, May, and December, decided so they wouldn't forget birthdays. Despite bleak conditions, their attitudes were gracious and grateful that Father Christmas found them.

"Ah, oui, the Chiasson family has been there for many years," Marceau said. "They kept to themselves, but every spring he came down to milk the goats. Did they truly name the babe 'December'?"

"I'm afraid that I started something, telling Flaxie about my favorite Christmas carol with its story of Good King Wenceslas' charitable heart."

"Well then, next Christmas, you must repeat the journey, or even better, bring them down by sleigh to enjoy Christmas at the Grand."

Ingrid's hand was on Bernard's arm. "I say it's time to build new traditions in the Wenceslas spirit. Oh yes, and later Flaxie must show you the coat Mrs. Chiasson gave her."

As if on cue, Flaxie arrived back. "Did you tell about the woodcutter?"

"I did indeed. I couldn't wait."

"And about the Wenceslas trip to town too?"

"Now that you're here, Flaxie, please do the honors."

She wiggled into a chair. "Uncle Bernard, with so much left from the buffet, we decided we could distribute the excess. In the Wenceslas spirit, many guests stepped forward, then dozens more from town. Together we delivered meals and treats to the hostel, train station, churches, and anyone we found in need. The staff pitched in on their own time and even led the street dancing festivities."

As Bernard listened, a spinning wheel of ideas churned in his brain.

"By golly, I can't believe I missed all this while I was away for not even three weeks. I've been richly blessed with rewards during my sabbatical, the greatest being my commitment to Ingrid. But the rest of you have amazed me.

"Logan, we can discuss business matters in my office in the morning after the breakfast session. Until we have new arrangements, please continue with your chef duties.

"And Flaxie, we need a separate business time. The Paris attorney will meet here next week as the distribution of your inheritance is imminent."

He struggled with the news of Ainsley but deferred.

"There is another pressing family matter for later. If there is nothing else now, we have a wedding to plan for New Year's Eve. We'll book the panorama sunroom for an intimate service, then we'll celebrate during the gala in the dining room's group alcove."

As Logan and Flaxie left, Ingrid called to her. "If you have time tomorrow, I'd be very pleased if you can help me with some arrangements."

Bernard smiled to himself, with a great burden lifted from his shoulders.

"Ingrid, all the puzzle pieces are falling into place one at a time."

"Yes, dear, they are. I'm glad to be the first piece in your complicated plan."

"Come now, Ernesto promised to hold the last carriage

A Wenceslas Christmas

for us. It's a full moon tonight and we can't miss a wish under the stars."

"Romance is in the air tonight, Flaxie. How about the disco for a nightcap? We have crossed our first hurdle. Tomorrow will be the second, then I'll deal with Paris and we can move on with our lives."

"Disco? Absolutely. I have too much on my mind tonight to expect I'd fall asleep. With four days to plan a wedding, we're going to be occupied but in an extraordinary way."

"As your uncle brought up your inheritance, I came across things accidentally in the great book. Have you ever heard a reference to a lodge?"

"In the back of my mind, yes. The adults talked about another lodge. You can show me what you found later."

"The Paris concierge gave me a message for your uncle, from some guy named Stanhope who said he'd be in town. I can't bring myself to disrupt his evening again with business."

"Hmm . . . Stanhope, it's oddly familiar."

Her mind flashed to an envelope addressed to Francesca from a convent in Venice in her mother's box.

In the elevator alone, Logan took her in his arms and pulled her against him, kissing her neck, her cheeks then her lips. "I love you, I love you, and I love you."

"When I'm with you, Logan, I forget the rest of the world and all is right. The next weeks will be hectic, but I will stand by you through thick and thin."

The elevator doors opened on the upper level. He did not leave the embrace, but looked out at the long line-up at the disco. Instead, he led her down the staircase back to the culinary room.

"I'll open a Beaujolais and we'll try your uncle's favorite

spot, the sunroom—I hear it's romantic."

On the way to the wine cellar, they passed the chef's office. "Logan, as we're here, can you show me the documents in the book?"

With the great book before her, she let her fingers fondle the aged leather strap.

"Father's hands must have been here many times. The pages are so fragile with age and wear."

"The lawyer's envelope is loose near the back and the architects' drawings and blueprints are midway."

23

Cards on the Table

Whistling to Gene Kelly's tune, 'I'm Getting Married in the Morning', Bernard's feet seemed lighter as he pranced into the kitchen at the end of the breakfast seating.

"Morning, everyone, you're a sight for sore eyes! It's good to be back."

"Congratulations, Chef Marceau, on your award in Paris," Magnon called out. "We had no doubts that you'd come out on top."

"Surely, it was not without obstacles, but I thank you for the encouragement, Magnon."

As the staff gathered around with congratulations, Roberto Dion bounded into the room.

"Chef Marceau, I'm hearing good things have happened and I regret that I wasn't here for it first-hand. I'm delighted about the upcoming nuptials with our precious Ingrid, and then your excellence at the chef's challenge. Is there more?"

"Roberto, you're the man I was looking for."

Bernard put his hand over his friend's shoulder and led him to the corner for a tête-à-tête.

"I apologize for not giving you the news directly as I returned unannounced last evening. Our wedding will be small and intimate on the night of the gala. I finally came to my senses being away, realizing what I have had in front of me all along. Would you do me the honor of standing with me?"

"Of course, Bernard. I have long wished for such an outcome between the two of you. Ingrid will be a beautiful bride and you will share years of happiness."

Marceau briefly outlined the intentions of the day to reserve the venues.

"I'll secure the rooms right away. May I take the liberty of coordinating it with Collins?"

"Proceed as you would with any wedding booking and let Ingrid know of the arrangements. She likes to know everything that is going on." Bernard chuckled at the irony. "But excuse me now, Roberto, I have a meeting scheduled with our chef."

Logan was early for the meeting with Marceau, with hope still fresh from Flaxie's message. He whispered it over and over as he waited. "Tell Logan that I've worked it out."

Marceau shook Dion's hand, then strode across the room with purpose. "Now, Logan, we'll have our chat. Come with me, the privacy of the chef's office would be more appropriate."

Bernard gestured to the open door and followed him to the leather sofa.

"Sit down, son, you're still the chef until we determine otherwise. First I congratulate you and thank you for maintaining the Grand's excellence of culinary services.

"While in Paris, I observed the environment in which you worked these past years, and I made some conclusions. I didn't make a lasting friendship with your Chef Augustus, and my assessment of the standards they set for the master chef was not to my liking.

"Without boring you with specifics, I discovered a scheme of cheating from other chefs' recipes. Chef Augustus used *your* cuttlefish recipe in the finale, and then I caught him red-handed trying to taint my sauces. He did place second ahead of Chef Lafrondière, but in my exit discussion with Morningside, I was frank in my opinion.

"I agreed not to make my observations of Augustus public in return for the immediate release from your sous-chef position on your approval, and I advised that the Grand Marceau would assume your employment. I deduced from my discussion with you that I had the liberty to speak for your termination, is that correct?"

Logan was pleased with the outcome and raised his eyebrows at the speed of it.

"With my nuptials and a honeymoon, I'll be busy, and you will carry on as head chef until I return. Beyond that are some major changes as Flaxie assumes more management. After I discuss the details with her, I'll outline the proposed growth plan here at the property.

"I won't leave you in limbo, Logan. Ingrid has confided in me about your romance with my niece. I think of her as my daughter, and if you go forward with a relationship with her, that will please me. Ultimately, her happiness is key to all my decisions, so our results are dependent on Flaxie."

Bernard's eyes searched Logan's reaction for the slightest muscle inflection.

"You know that Flaxie will speak from her heart when

you approach her," Logan said. "I have spoken to her and I do not see my future without her. Last week by phone, you advised me that I should fight for her and not consider her financial status. I'm not interested in benefiting in any way from Flaxie other than winning her love."

Bernard nodded. "I wish I were a young romantic again to have more time with Ingrid. You are right to pursue your heart. In the coming days, complicated business aspects will be resolved including Flaxie's inheritance. In Paris, I met with her father's attorney and it will be necessary for her to settle some papers.

"The attorneys will come to Mont Blanc to finalize details, but there's another sensitive matter and I don't mind broaching it with you for your viewpoint. It was revealed to me that Flaxie's mother had a child before her marriage to my brother. I won't belabor the details, but my lawyer Willoughby is arranging for the lad to come and meet his half-sister."

"I am grateful for your interceding with the King George on my behalf. Thank you for the explanation. I know that you are a man of astute wisdom and trust, whatever you decide. As far as Flaxie having a half-brother, I believe it will give her great pleasure to discover a long lost sibling."

In an after-thought, Logan passed the phone message about Ainsley Stanhope across the desk. Marceau opened it before proceeding to find Dion.

"Roberto, I need a discreet favor."

Marceau took the photo from his pocket and gave Dion a glimpse.

"I haven't seen this chap," Dion said, examining the face. "Sir, if he comes to the hotel, you'll be the first to know. Should I be aware of his name?"

A Wenceslas Christmas 171

Marceau hesitated at first. "He might say it's Stanhope."

"Stanhope! Why someone called the other day and used that name."

"What did he want?"

"He said he'd be a guest at Flaxie's birthday party and wanted to know the arrangements. Of course, I had no information to give him."

Bernard was taken off guard and pocketed the picture again. "I expect we'll be seeing him then."

Flaxie and Ingrid dallied over the guest lists and the sunroom's seating arrangements. In short order, they decided on flowers and musicians, and Flaxie offered to phone around for an officiant and a photographer.

"You know, Ingrid, the most important detail is your wedding dress. Do you have something in mind?"

"I've been thumbing through bride magazines and found a dress at Bergman's in Grenoble. I called and they agreed to ship it in time. It's a mid-calf ivory silk sheath fitted with cap sleeves. I'm not one for too much frill."

Flaxie jumped up and grabbed Ingrid by the hand. "Come up to the apartment. Mother had most of Grandmother Marceau's jewelry and I know she would want you to wear something borrowed."

"Are you sure?"

Half an hour later, Roberto Dion sent a bell boy to find Flaxie and Ingrid at the penthouse.

Marceau was waiting in the chef's office poring over a file of documents when Flaxie entered with a sheepish grin.

"I'm sorry we were difficult to find. I took Ingrid to mother's room for something borrowed . . . it's time for the talk, isn't it?"

Settling back in his armchair, he sighed. "Yes, my dear.

Since you don't appear surprised, I'll assume you know about the estate. It is due on your birthday and has accumulated a significant value. The lawyer in Paris has been handling your affairs in trust. You'll assume fifty percent control of the Grand Marceau and become my full partner.

"Feel free to move into the penthouse apartment where you can connect to your memories. Ingrid and I will be down the hall. Willoughby, the family attorney, will come at the end of next week with paperwork. And think about what you might like as a comfortable living allowance. I hope I am not presumptive to assume that you will remain here to help run the business."

"Oh, of course, Uncle Bernard, this is my home. But tell me, what is 'Mistletoe Lodge'?"

"You know about that too? Many years ago my father discussed a plan to expand the hotel as the need became apparent. The site is on the hill overlooking the main hotel where the goats graze. We hoped to build a conference facility and funicular to join the two sites.

"Should the time come that we had another chef, it would be reasonable to proceed and divide the responsibilities."

"Let's focus on your wedding, for now, Uncle, then we'll deal with Willoughby and the business matters before my birthday. Perhaps then we'll talk of your blueprints for . . . 'Wenceslas Chateau'. You do know I love Logan with all my heart. I've never had another feeling like this."

"I'm truly thrilled for you, Flaxie, and yes, Wenceslas Chateau has a nice ring. In the last few days, that tune has been running through my head continually."

In the throes of preparations, Flaxie decided on a trip to Chamonix to shop a few days after Christmas. The impromptu excursion was a welcome escape and opportunity to hunt for a wedding gift for her uncle.

Strolling across the bridge near rue du Docteur Paccard, she was enticed by the window displays of designer apparel and stopped to select new shoes, a handbag, and a matching pair of alpine, ceramic steins. On a seat at an outside patio, she sipped a cup of Lindt hot chocolate and looked up at the pristine beauty of Mont Blanc.

"My goodness, the Grand Marceau looks magnificent from here, with its hundreds of years of history and memories for thousands. I am so blessed. I'll capture this vision in my memory forever. It looks like a fairytale castle."

24

New Year's Eve

Fresh snowflakes had created a fairyland on the morning of New Year's Eve, and by sunrise, the sunroom was bustling with preparations for the ceremony with decorations, chair covers, and satin bows.

Flaxie, Juliette, Marianne, and Helene, her long-time housekeeping supervisor, coerced Ingrid to a morning sipping mimosas in the spa, with manicures, makeup, and hairdos in the peaceful ambiance of a classical violin serenade.

"Tell us what you're thinking, Ingrid?" Marianne said. "You can say anything among the girls."

Tittering, Ingrid blushed. "This is a magical day when all my dreams will come true. Bernard is my prince and I will love him for eternity. Besides a husband, I get a wonderful family and cherished friends. I am truly blessed besides starting to feel a bit tipsy and I'm curious about which of you will catch my bouquet."

Her eyes followed to Flaxie then Marianne, both pleased with the suggestion.

Roberto stayed attentive to the details as he carefully opened the morning's delivery of white and pink roses to complement the outfits. Standing in the ballroom with his arms crossed, he admired his efforts.

Collins and his crew were preparing the ballroom for the midnight events, bringing out pizzazz, noisemakers, party hats, garlands, and streamers from the ceiling.

A flurry of commotion and jitters consumed most of the day. Amid activities, Flaxie and Logan hadn't even spoken until 2 p.m. when she barged into the kitchen to find him.

"Logan! You're not dressed for the wedding."

"Neither are you. Magnon will finish here for me and I'll be gone, I promise."

She rushed a kiss to his cheek and flew back out the dining room door toward the elevator.

Bernard rang the reception manager at the front desk to remind Roberto to rendezvous in the sunroom.

"He's already there waiting, Chef Marceau."

Leaving his apartment for the last time as a bachelor, he stopped at the door and took an umbrella from the stand and gave it a twirl.

"I'm off to get my Missus."

Standing with Dion, the lyrist began the processional, Vivaldi's Allegro, as Ingrid and Flaxie entered carrying cascades of roses. Logan was taken aback at the vision of his girl in a dusty rose strapless poi de soie gown, with Ingrid at her side, an apparition of ivory and pearls.

On a backdrop of the golden evening sun filtering into the room, the couple declared their vows of eternal love.

Following an eruption of applause, the priest called out his announcement, "Monsieur Bernard et Madame Ingrid Marceau".

Roberto interrupted the rounds of hugs and kisses. "I'm sorry, folks, but the photographer is on the clock. We must go now to the atrium for portraits."

Logan slipped away to the kitchen and exchanged his suit jacket for the chef's apron, then checked his notes for hors d'oeuvres for the reception and for special orders for the New Year's Eve feast.

"Chef Powell, we are overbooked it seems," Collins said. "I don't know how it happened."

"Fix it with staff, then. See if the front can spare people, or extend overtime. I'll approve it."

Marianne and Juliette came right away. "Logan, we heard of the dilemma. How can we help?"

"Thankfully you're here. Get the numbers from Collins so Ernesto and Philippe can set up extra tables. There's plenty of food. Where is Hunter?"

"He'll make it for the reception but couldn't get time off. At New Year's the ranger station is always understaffed."

Seconds later, Flaxie arrived with an update. "The bride and groom have gone to change for the reception."

"Flaxie, I neglected to say how beautiful you are today," Logan said with a grin. "And can you check the settings and flowers?"

"Yes, Chef." She gestured a salute and threw a kiss.

As the last patron left the dining room, the beat of the ballroom band started up.

But in the ballroom's elegant, soundproof side room, trays of champagne flutes were circulating to tables as Bernard and Ingrid arrived.

A Wenceslas Christmas 177

For the informal, intimate reception, Ingrid requested a traditional Austrian meal with a mushroom schnitzel, spaetzle, and braised red cabbage. Logan expanded it to four courses with the background of classical flute, violin, and oboe.

She felt she owed Logan an explanation for rejecting his gourmet options. "It's been many years, but it's a memory of my childhood that is important to embrace."

Roberto toasted their happiness and longevity, then Bernard raved about his long-time relationship with Ingrid and his realization that his soulmate had always been at his side.

"I told a friend in Paris that without her I'd lost my left foot—that's when I knew I'd been an old fool. Ingrid has not only been my guide and shadow, but also my conscience. She often knows me better than I do myself."

With the tinkling of glasses, they embraced like teenagers.

Marianne's mind was on Hunter, and her eyes gave it away as they drifted to the doorway.

"Perhaps he thinks you caught the bouquet and he got cold feet," Flaxie teased.

"Hunter wouldn't get cold feet as we've had long talks. But I wonder what delayed him. It must be important as he wouldn't miss this."

From the doorway, Ernesto got the attention of Dion, then delivered a folded message to be passed to Logan.

S.O.S. from woodcutter's cabin. Due to heavy snow, I'll take the dog sled team from First Aid station and the intern on duty. I have strobe lights for signaling – blue okay, red send help.

As the guests moved to the ballroom for the Marceau's

first dance, Logan shared the note with Flaxie.

"I don't need to ruin your uncle's evening or dampen tonight's spirit," he whispered. "I'd like permission to take a rescue snowmobile up the mountain."

"When?"

"I'll load supplies now and be back by midnight. Can you post someone to watch for strobe light signals?"

"Under other circumstances, I'd come with you, Logan. Take a walkie-talkie from Ernesto and I'll find an excuse for Uncle Bernard."

Hans volunteered to stand to watch as the ski lift was closed. The snowmobile's tail lights faded into the tree line. With binoculars, he watched high on the hill for Hunter's strobe lights but saw only darkness.

25

Logan Goes Missing

A half-hour turned into one hour, then two, and Hans still waited for any signal. Flaxie's anxiety became fear when she checked on him at 11:30.

"One of them should be back by now or at least have some communication, Hans. I'm worried. The snow is too heavy now."

"Perhaps it's time to tell Monsieur Marceau."

Marceau was in the middle of a slow waltz with his bride, but Flaxie knew it was time to alert him. The walk across the ballroom floor seemed an eternity and she was startled when she heard her name.

"Flaxie!"

Turning, she was disappointed to see Hunter Bodine alone. Marianne bounced over to him.

"Where's Logan?"

"What do you mean? I haven't seen Logan. I waved the

blue strobe to indicate all was clear. Maybe he couldn't see it through the snow. I just got back with the doctor and we'll follow-up in the next few days. Madame should be okay for now."

Without flinching, Flaxie said, "How could you leave him out there? He went to help you."

"Calm down, Flaxie!" Marianne snapped in defense. "It's not Hunter's fault." The raised voices brought Bernard from the party.

"What's going on? It's midnight when we should all be hugging and kissing."

As Flaxie relayed the scenario, Ernesto reported to them. "I tracked the GPS on the ATV. It isn't moving but I have a location. I'll round up a crew and we'll find him."

"This can't be happening," Ingrid said. Bernard suddenly stood taller as he took charge.

"Hunter, you know the terrain best. Take the lead but minimize the risks with no more than six in the rescue party. The halogen lanterns in the generator room are powerful through the blinding snow. And set the tracking beacon on a loud decibel."

Flaxie leaned into Ingrid's arms. "I have to go, you know. I need to find him."

"Dear, you are best to wait here with us, it's dark and dangerous. The ranger is the best guide. They'll find him and he'll be back in no time."

"Ingrid is right, Flaxie," Bernard said. "He could turn up here any time under his own power."

With the bitter wind howling, and visibility reduced to a few meters, the convoy escalated the hill behind Hunter. Ernesto maintained the tracking and within an hour they located the beeping from the snowmobile.

A Wenceslas Christmas

In snowshoes and with a lantern on his head, Hans plodded toward the trees where the brush was too dense and snow too deep for vehicles.

"Logan, Logan Powell, are you there?" he called.

"I can see part of the trailer," Hunter yelled.

He shone the halogen into the bush. "It's still loaded with supplies . . . ahead by those boulders."

The rescuers repeatedly called Logan's name as the gusts whipped their words. Hunter spread his men out in a horizontal line and proceeded forward with eyes on the ground.

"Over there," Hans called, "the red parka in the snow. He's trapped under his ATV, it's on its side."

The medic pressed through the deep snow. "

He's unresponsive . . . his pulse is good but he's unconscious. Bring the blankets."

Hunter was on his knee beside his friend. "Logan, we've got you, you'll be alright. Looks like you knocked yourself out in a spill."

Groggily, Logan answered. "Flaxie, I need to be back for midnight."

At the Grand, the revelry was dying down, with the lobby littered with streamers and party favors.

In a half-hearted effort, a group of night staffers and cleaners began sweeping the remnants, and at the Christmas tree, other faithful staff waited solemnly for word of the rescue.

A sudden gust of cold air brought Dion in from the veranda and every head turned in suspense.

"I can see them now with the binoculars. They're coming down . . . there are six sets of headlights."

Flaxie ran back with him to see for herself. Ernesto was

maneuvering the lead vehicle with two others behind him tooting a warning horn. Behind that, Hunter pulled a rescue sleigh piled high with blankets.

Hunter yelled to Flaxie with a thumbs up "Ahoy! He's here." Watching from the door, Ingrid rushed out with a coat for Flaxie, and Bernard carried another blanket.

Hunter intercepted Flaxie as she charged across the lane.

"It appears he has a concussion. The ATV hit a boulder and threw him. We should take him to the emergency maison in Chamonix, but I know it only has skeleton staff tonight. Is the house doctor in?"

"I'll get Marianne. It's getting colder by the minute. Bring him in to get warmed up. Use the guest room in my parent's penthouse suite."

Hunter looked for Bernard's reaction. "Is that okay?"

"Do whatever Flaxie has asked, Hunter," Marceau said. "Keep him safe and warm."

At the gurney, she loosened the scarf that protected Logan's face and carefully brushed the new snow that had gathered. She dabbed the bleeding gash on his forehead and rubbed his cheeks until his eyes fluttered.

"I'm here, Logan. I'm going to get you better, that's a promise."

Bernard laid a reassuring hand on her shoulder.

"Logan Powell, we need you to get better for the sake of this family."

"Follow me," Ingrid piped up. "We'll use the faster service elevator inside the kitchen door. It goes there directly."

"Marianne, go as well and attend to Logan," Bernard said. "Roberto can round up more medical help. I've heard you're an excellent nurse . . . and midwife too. We rarely need a midwife, but having in-house medical is underrated."

A Wenceslas Christmas

As the men carried Logan on the rescue board, Flaxie held his hand. His speech was incoherent and she listened for any clarity. Ingrid was primping the guest bed when the team arrived.

"I have an appointment with Chef Marceau," he said. "I can't be late for it and forfeit my opportunity. His beautiful daughter . . ." His words halted and his eyes opened as he struggled with reality.

"Logan, you'll be alright. Don't worry about the appointment, you have the position."

His face contorted with confusion as he fought to focus on the sound of voices.

Ernesto and Hunter eased him out of his ski suit and laid him on the mattress, barely conscious.

"I can't see the Eiffel tower from here . . ."

Flaxie covered her mouth in alarm as it was obvious he had lost his memory.

"Logan, it's me, your Flaxie. You must remember, please try."

His eyes were blank and closed again as his head sunk back onto the pillow.

Ingrid stepped forward to console her.

"Dear, this is not uncommon with a head injury. The doctor will be here soon and you should let him rest. Time will be the best healer. I'll have the Morris chair brought here from the parlor and set beside his bed. We'll take turns sitting with him and send word to you as soon as he is cognizant."

"Ingrid is right," Bernard said. "It's almost two in the morning. I'll ask the doctor to give you a sedative so you can sleep."

"No sedative. I'm not leaving! I know you want the best for me, but this is my decision. You should be enjoying your honeymoon. Please, Uncle Bernard, you and Ingrid should go."

They agreed, but Bernard still looked back with concern. As they reached the door, the doctor arrived.

"Come in, doctor, and thank you," Flaxie said. "I'm sorry for interrupting your New Years at this hour, but we need your help."

"I've attended to the Marceau family for many years and I never once stopped to check to see what time it was or ever considered it an interruption."

His eyes wandered back to Bernard. "Ah, Monsieur Marceau et Madame Ingrid, congratulations on the splendid news of your wedding."

"Thank you, Edward. We're grateful for your attendance tonight. Logan is a special person to my niece. Marianne here says it's a concussion—she has medical training as a nurse."

"Then I must see to the young man at once. Marianne, perhaps you might like to assist me."

Flaxie clung to Logan's hand as he drifted in and out of sleep.

"Apart from bruises, I don't detect any broken bones. Vitals are stable but there's a strong indication of trauma. I'll dress the head wound—it isn't too deep."

"He doesn't seem to remember me at all, doctor, and I don't understand why he doesn't respond to my voice or touch."

"My dear Flaxie, healing is a process and you can't expect immediate results. The brain recovers during sleep. Don't overstimulate it by making him think too hard. Concussions generally have a full recovery but it could be seven or ten days or longer. With luck, it'll be faster.

"The best results are when the afflicted is surrounded by family and a familiar environment. No caffeine or sugar, but

A Wenceslas Christmas

when he's ready to eat, keep him on healthy food, like dairy and fruits and vegetables.

"If you prefer, would you like me to make arrangements at the hospital?"

"No, he must remain here with us."

26

Recovered Plans

The sun filtered through the curtains causing Flaxie to stir in the Morris chair. As she awoke, her eyes shifted to the bed where Logan lay unaware of how much time had elapsed.

With a light tap and a cheerful voice, Ingrid let herself in carrying a breakfast tray. "Good morning! How's the patient?"

"I guess I fell asleep," Flaxie whispered. She leaned over Logan. "His breathing is even but otherwise there's little change."

"Your uncle made your favorite crêpes and insists that you eat. Flaxie. Also, I brought a protein breakfast for dear Logan—a hard-boiled egg, a variety of cheeses, an apple, and a glass of milk. Do your best when he wakes, Sweetheart. I'll put the kettle on for tea for the two of us."

Minutes later the door tapped again.

"My shift now," Marianne said. "Flaxie, take a shower or go to bed and I'll wake you in a few hours. You don't want him to wake up seeing and you fraught and drained. Take some time to yourself."

Flaxie accepted the suggestion to freshen up, and returning minutes later, she found Bernard waiting to check on her.

"Bonjour, ma chèrie. Any improvement? Dion says the doctor will be up in a few minutes."

"Uncle Bernard, I'm so worried. He hasn't even moved through the night."

"That must be good that he is resting well."

She smiled wistfully. "Pshaw, as Grandmama used to say, you're twisting the situation so I won't see the truth."

With a damp cloth, she wiped Logan's brow and rubbed his cheeks, then planted a kiss on his forehead. Sitting on the edge of his bed, she held his hand.

"Logan, I love you. Please wake up."

Seconds later, she gasped. "Uncle Bernard, I'm certain that I felt him squeeze my hand."

The doctor heard her as he arrived. "That's welcome news indeed. Marianne, help me prop him up. The change in position will improve his circulation. Can you make the changes every hour? If he doesn't eat or drink on his own, I'll put in an intravenous tube."

From a reflex test, Logan emitted a few groans. "Ah, that's much better, Monsieur Powell."

His eyes fluttered as he surveyed his surroundings. "Where am I? What happened?"

As Flaxie leaned to speak, Bernard cautioned her and stepped in front.

"Please, let me first. Logan, do you know me?"

"Yes, Sir, I know from the Michelin magazine. You are

the head chef on Mont Blanc."

His eyes went to the beautiful blonde watching him intently.

"Do you know anyone else in this room?"

Puzzling and straining, he studied Marianne, Flaxie, and Ingrid, then eased back onto the pillow exhausted. "They are all lovely but I'm afraid not. The pretty one with the flaxen hair looks at me with pain in her eyes."

Logan raised his head. "Wait . . . flaxen . . . Flaxie . . ."

Satisfied with his effort, the doctor tried simple queries of his name, where he was and the date, but Logan hesitated on all of them.

"You did well and we'll try again later. For now, we need you to rest but first, you should eat and drink something. Will you try?"

"Yes, I'm thirsty. Ingrid, can I have an expresso?" Logan gasped. "I remember someone saying that."

Bernard, Ingrid, and Flaxie couldn't help but laugh.

"You are remembering. I'm Ingrid and I do make an espresso every morning for Bernard. You have heard me say that."

Logan nodded pretending he understood. "I'd still like an espresso." Again they laughed and he seemed pleased.

The doctor reminded them, "No caffeine, for now, folks. Sorry." He excused himself, to return later.

"I'll see you out, Edward," Ingrid said.

Logan's eyes settled again on Flaxie. "I believe you rescued me from the avalanche, didn't you?"

"The avalanche was weeks ago. You've been here at the hotel for three weeks as head chef. In that time you and I have become very close."

As Logan thought about that, Bernard said, "We need you to get better, Logan. Do you remember our discussions about your future here?"

His brow tightened and he pulled himself up to a sitting position.

"My head is jumbled fog, but I remember bits and pieces. I'm sure it will sort itself out. The dark-haired girl . . . you are Marianne. I've known you for a while."

"Logan, I've been your assistant while you were sous-chef in Paris. You're a rising career chef and the culinary world is your passion. Maybe you remember Flaxie and the mission up the mountain to the woodcutter's cabin. Do you remember Wenceslas?"

Powell began to hum 'Good King Wenceslas'. "I love that song. Yes, the woodcutter's cabin . . . we went with sleighs to the cabin with the little girls. It was December."

"Four of us went," Marianne said. "I was with Hunter, the ranger? And you and Flaxie were together."

The interaction was painful for Flaxie. She rose to leave the bedside, then looked back as he hadn't released her hand. "Don't go."

Bernard put his hand on Flaxie's shoulder.

"Sweetheart, I'm needed downstairs. You'll be fine here with Logan. Watch him improve and call me if you need me. And Chef Powell, I'll need you back on your feet soon as I'd like to reschedule my honeymoon."

"Honeymoon!"

Suddenly more facts donned on Logan. "I'm sorry. Of course, Monsieur Marceau, you married espresso Ingrid."

"Yes, espresso Ingrid. For now, I'll return to the chef's duties until you are well. Don't take too long. Shortly, a light lunch will be sent up for you."

Flaxie kiss his forehead. "I hope that you will remember me soon, and remember us."

With his eyes closed, he concentrated on the scent of her

hair, the touch of her lips, and the tenderness of her soft voice.

"Flaxie! I can tell you've had pain in your life and I won't cause you more. Bit by bit, faces and events are making more sense. I'll find myself again if you can be patient with me."

She laid her head on his shoulder, and he stroked her hair.

"I missed our New Year's Eve kiss under the mistletoe," she said. "You went out to follow Hunter up the mountain. I wanted to go with you."

His eyes widened. "Mistletoe? Mistletoe Lodge?"

Laughing, she said, "Oh yes, Logan, but remember we decided it should be the Wenceslas Chateau instead."

"I like the sound of that."

"Seafood lunch is ready for the patient from Chef Marceau," Ingrid called from the door. "I'll put it on the nightstand."

"It smells so good. I'll try to sit up at the table."

"I'm afraid it's not a good idea with your headache," Ingrid said. "We don't know how your legs are going to respond."

"His legs are strong enough," Flaxie said. "Logan first arrived at the hotel with a badly sprained ankle. It was so swollen he couldn't stand, but the two of us managed to get him to his room."

Logan's brows raised. "That's not quite right, Flaxie. A man from the concierge helped, but you were my accomplice when I arrived."

The pair laughed at their dilemma. Strengthened with determination, he pulled himself up, then laid his arm over her shoulder for support and took a few steps to regain his balance.

Flaxie moved the tray to the table and sat across as he ate.

A Wenceslas Christmas

"This is good . . . yes, I remember that this was on the menu for today. I messed up going up the hill in the dark on my own."

"I'm just glad you are remembering. I want you back."

27

Stanhope Connection

In Chamonix, Ranger Bodine posted a help wanted sign on the billboard outside the hostel. A few guests loitered in the morning sunshine, including Ainsley Stanhope, who was leaving to find a bistro for a cup of coffee.

"Bonjour, Ranger, is that for a job? What do you need?"

Bodine was struck by something in the lad's appearance. "Have we met before? You seem familiar."

"I don't remember meeting you, but I know you are a village hero. Tales of the woodcutter rescue are still talked about in the bars and cafes. I saw you at the hostel during the Christmas Eve drive. Is there a position available?"

"Yes, in fact, there is. The season is so busy and I've lost my best snow dog trainer and guide. Do you have any experience in that field?"

Ainsley knew he would have to lie to convince Bodine.

Looking the ranger in the eye, he said, "I could tell you

that I'm skilled with dogs and driving sleds in the Alps, but if you hired me you'd find out soon enough that it was an exaggeration. Apart from my lack of experience, I'm eager to learn and in good health. My outdoor endurance is superb."

Hunter laughed at his candor.

"Thanks for cutting to the chase. Give it a few days and I'll see if anyone with skills comes forward. If not, I'm willing to provide training for the right person. I'll need to take a spare dog sled team up the mountain by the end of the week, and I can't drive two teams at once. I'm in a bit of a fix."

Ainsley sighed, relieved that his quip wasn't rejected.

"I'll be here if you need me. They call me Ainsley."

Hunter gave a thumbs up and moved on down the main street to post more ads as the kid watched from the hostel overcome with desperation. After they were tacked up, the newcomer removed them to improve his chances.

In the afternoon, Ainsley introduced himself to a local gallery near the bridge and negotiated with the owner to hang his Alpine paintings for a short while.

"I can't promise anything, Monsieur, but they are beautifully vibrant. You must have been painting in the Alps for a while to have this depth of expression. Leave them for a few weeks on consignment and we'll see if there's interest."

With the doctor's consent and an improvement in his memory, Logan returned to his room. Sleeping soundly, the last three weeks were sorting out within his thoughts and he was at greater peace.

The next morning, he surprised everyone when he strode into the kitchen where Chef Marceau was in charge. He looked refreshed with only a small camouflage dressing over the wound on his forehead.

"Good morning, Chef, how can I be of assistance?"

Bernard was startled. "My dear boy, does Flaxie know you are up and around?"

"Of course she does. She's gone to find Ingrid."

At first, Marceau shook his head with a leery expression. "I'll need the doctor's permission for you to return. But if he gives his okay, we'll take our honeymoon on a Danube Cruise. I want to see her homeland, Austria."

"I'll take care of the doctor's paperwork today and I'll plan to return to my duties tomorrow, Sir."

Preparing for Willoughby's arrival, Marceau and Flaxie pored over the legal documents in his office.

"We will host them well and they can return to Paris for the legwork," he said. "Considering the significance of this birthday, we'll have another spectacular celebration."

"The events have moved so quickly, Uncle Bernard. If Logan proposes, I will say yes, and then following in your footsteps, I don't want a long engagement. We will want to live in the penthouse apartment with a few renovations and continue here with our responsibilities.

"I'd like to see the investments enhance the Grand Marceau and actively advance with the Wenceslas Chateau. With two master chefs, surely another Michelin star will be forthcoming. I hope you'll be able to enjoy decreased work in the future to spend more time with Ingrid. The hotel's reputation will always rely on your culinary direction."

"I appreciate your diplomacy, Flaxie, and cajoling my ego. Now that Ingrid and I are married, I'll need leisure and travel time. I also promised her a weekend in Paris in the spring. But first, let's deal with Willoughby and have a birthday party of all parties."

"No, Uncle Bernard, a quiet dinner with just family. I

don't want a big fuss, really I don't."

As Bernard returned to the kitchen, Flaxie stayed to study the documents alone, stopping at notations in the Grand Marceau's great livre.

Her interest was heightened at her father's notes in his handwriting, especially at family tree details she hadn't seen.

Frederick Eugene Marceau married Francesca Therese Stanhope on January 16, 1990, at Grenoble.

First born son, Frederick Xavier Marceau, delivered stillborn at Argentière on November 3, 1990, buried St. Mark's cemetery, Chamonix.

Second born daughter, Francesca Gabrielle Marceau at the Grand Hotel, Mont Blanc, January 25, 1992.

Shocked to learn she had a brother who died at birth, she sat back to digest it.

"I'd forgotten that my mother's maiden name was Stanhope, that's where I've heard it before. I must find that envelope from the convent! What was it that Logan asked me?"

She paused, confused. "If he'd lived, I would have experienced a sibling to share and treasure without my loneliness. And he'd be heir to my father's estate. But why have I not heard of this before? Uncle Bernard has kept many secrets from me. What else is hidden in these pages?"

Hours later, Logan found Flaxie still absorbed in documents and notes. She looked like she'd been awakened from a dream.

"Ingrid has been looking for you."

"I didn't realize time had passed. Logan, why did you ask me if I'd heard the name Stanhope?"

"A message came to your uncle. I shouldn't have said

anything."

"But I'm glad that you did. It's in my family tree . . . Stanhope is Mother's maiden name. Curious that it came up for Uncle Bernard in Paris."

She sauntered to the doorway to Logan and slid her arms around him. Gazing into the magical eyes that first swept her heart, she said, "I can't wait for this pressure to be over and we can enjoy being ourselves. Willoughby is coming in a few days, then Uncle Bernard and Ingrid will leave at last for their honeymoon."

He whispered, "When your uncle returns, let's elope and go to the sunny beaches of Marseille for a weekend. I promise it will be romantic and the beginning of a wonderful life together. To appease the staff and family, we can host a reception here later."

"I love you so much, Logan. The idea is perfect . . . and the Mediterranean. Yes, let's get married soon."

To prepare for Willoughby's team, Marceau described the attorneys to Dion who would meet and transfer them from the train.

"Roberto, while they are here we might also have a drop-in guest. He's a lad about Logan's age with blond, curly hair and unmistakable blue eyes like Francesca's. He might introduce himself as Ainsley Hayhurst or Stanhope."

"Presumably he will not be staying as a hotel guest but it's more of an appointment, is that correct?"

"Quite, but we'll see how it goes. However for now, please keep the matter to yourself."

"Certainly."

As Marceau turned to retreat, Hunter Bodine arrived out of breath in search of Marianne.

"Good day, Hunter. Marianne is in the kitchen. You

A Wenceslas Christmas

know your way."

"Thank you, Sir. I've hired a lad from the hostel in Chamonix and we're going to take the extra dog sled team up to the Chaisson place."

"Excellent, see Logan for supplies as you need. And send our best wishes to the woodcutter. Tell him I'll look for him with the goats in the spring."

Willoughby and Singleton arrived on cue and settled into their rooms. In no time, they took over a conference room off the mezzanine level as their working base.

"Welcome, Benoit and Milton. We are glad to entertain you here, delighted that you made the trip to the mountain air of Mont Blanc. Surely you'll find this a pleasant diversion from the city's pace."

Two more accomplices were behind the attorneys and Marceau gestured politely to welcome them too.

Benoit was ready to get to the business. "Thank you, Bernard. We'll get ourselves organized. Can we meet, say early afternoon, with you and Flaxie?"

"That can be arranged. Two o'clock?"

"Good. Bernard, the matter regarding the Stanhope lad is still in the mill. I expect to hear from him today as he claims to be in the area."

"Yes, yes. I'll prepare Flaxie for it."

Flaxie and Marianne were packing food supplies for Hunter when Marceau entered the kitchen.

"The attorneys have arrived, Flaxie. We have a two o'clock meeting, but I need to have a word with you now."

Marceau led her to his office. A solemn expression crossed his face and Flaxie knew she needed to take a chair.

"What is it?

"When I was with Willoughby in Paris, I was enlightened

about an old secret that my brother kept." Marceau went on to elaborate on the details that had been confided regarding Francesca's child.

It took a few minutes to absorb the news of a long lost sibling. Marceau allowed her time and was both cautious and curious about her response.

"Uncle Bernard, this is wonderful. I have the brother I always wanted and now I can share all my memories of Mother with this man. Where is he?"

"He has been in contact with Willoughby who will set up a meeting here at the hotel. It seems the lad is in Chamonix already."

"Then he uses the name Stanhope, doesn't he? Mother's maiden name."

"Yes, Ainsley Stanhope, but also his adoptive father's surname Hayhurst."

"Then when we meet with Willoughby, I'll have a few more questions."

The two o'clock meeting began academically around intense details of investments and restructured dividends. Flaxie proved to be a prudent financial student and made copious notes and queries before mentioning the chateau land.

"The land is freehold and held by the corporation," Singleton said, "with decisions to be made by its primary shareholders, you and Bernard. The only legal aspects are the deed and land survey for you to proceed with development."

"We've covered most facets of the Marceau estate, however, I'm curious if Mother had any Stanhope assets. If she did, understandably Ainsley is entitled to a portion."

Benoit raised his eyebrows. "Yes, you're right, Flaxie. When married people perish in the same tragedy, it is necessary to determine which died first. Regretfully, this will be painful to hear, but it was your mother. Therefore, the few assets she'd acquired went into Frederick's estate.

"Your father was aware of Francesca's child and left instruction for him to be paid a settlement. When Monsieur Hayhurst contacted us in Paris, he was informed of that bequest and we will complete the transaction shortly."

"That is good. Father always saw the best in people."

Ernesto tapped at the conference door. "A message for Monsieur Marceau."

"Mon dear Uncle Bernard, would it be possible to join you and your colleagues for dinner this evening at the hotel? I am otherwise engaged until after 7 p.m. with employment."

Bernard burst into boisterous laughter. "Uncle Bernard, he says!"

"Ernesto, is the lad waiting for a reply?"

"No, he was not able to remain as he had other duties. He said he would check this afternoon for an answer."

"Did he look particularly hungry?" Marceau toyed.

"I suppose so. He was rather slight but curly, blond hair like your niece."

"Very well, tell him to join us at seven."

28

Lost is Found

Ingrid and Bernard hosted a private dinner in the alcove for the legal team and Ainsley Hayhurst. Willoughby's team was accustomed to precise clockwork and were seated ten minutes before 7 p.m. to start cocktails.

Logan escorted Flaxie into the dining room in a stunning indigo blue evening dress selected from Francesca's wardrobe.

Marceau's jaw dropped. "My Lord, I remember that dress. You are a vision of our beautiful Francesca, Flaxie. It's an honor that you wear it."

"Oh yes, Flaxie, it is like seeing a ghost yet even more lovely," Ingrid added. "Those pearls were a wedding gift to her from your father."

"I felt the need to connect with sentiment for this meeting with Ainsley. I have so much to tell him."

At five past seven, Dion escorted Hayhurst, wearing the

same apparel as he wore when he met at Willoughby's Paris office.

"Would you be inclined to borrow one of our house dinner jackets, Monsieur Hayhurst?" Roberto asked.

"No, I need no disguise."

"If I may say, Monsieur, you have an uncanny resemblance to your mother."

"So the word is about regarding my family ties."

"Chamonix and Mont Blanc represent a tight community and rumors abound. I apologize if that has inconvenienced you."

All eyes went to the alcove entrance as Dion made the introduction.

"Monsieur Ainsley Stanhope-Hayhurst."

The young man stepped forward with a half-smile and an awkward, extended hand. "The great Marceau, I'm delighted to finally meet you."

He was focused on the flaxen-haired woman in the blue dress. "You are Flaxie Marceau, I've seen your picture. I'd heard that you have remarkable features like my mother."

"I'm sorry that I didn't know of you until recently. You do understand however that Mother never knew what happened to you as the convent sealed the adoption file."

Bernard was startled that Flaxie knew of the boy.

"You see, Uncle Bernard, I've become a bit of a sleuth to uncover my family tree. Mother left a box of old letters in the apartment so I made the connection."

"Welcome to the Grand, Ainsley, please make yourself comfortable. I'm Ingrid, Flaxie's aunt." Ingrid twittered at the odd sound of her words.

"Congratulations are in order, Ingrid," he answered. "I heard in Chamonix that New Year's Eve was particularly exciting at the hotel."

"Have you been in Chamonix long?" Flaxie asked.

"I came up Christmas Eve arriving in time to see your Wenceslas outreach. I'm an obliging guest at the local hostel."

Marceau was stunned to learn of his circumstances.

"Ainsley, there's no need for you to remain in those quarters. We have extra space in our staff rooms and you are welcome to remain at the hotel as long as you need."

Logan wasn't sure if Ainsley's reaction was in humiliation or burned pride. His face reddened and he looked away, softly accepting the invitation.

"I intend to pay my way, Monsieur Marceau. I have recently obtained employment with the alpine unit."

"The alpine unit? Ah, you are the new dog sled trainer Bodine was telling me about. My congratulations."

Flaxie was curious about her sibling's plans. "Are you planning to remain in Chamonix? I have many fond memories of Mother that I can share with you. It would be nice to have more family in the vicinity."

"My passion is to be an artist. In Montparnasse, it was a struggle to find a market for my work, but when I came to the Alps I was smitten with the beauty. And I've painted every day. I have a renewed energy that I hope will show in my work."

"I heard in the village that a new artist is in town from Paris," Flaxie said. "I'd like to see your paintings."

Ainsley looked to Logan. "And are you a Marceau too?"

"No, I'm Flaxie's fiancé."

"My congratulations—it seems you're a lucky man. I look forward to getting to know you."

The interaction between Flaxie and Ainsley impressed and amused Marceau at the resemblance. At Ingrid's encouragement, he posed the invitation.

"Flaxie's birthday celebration is next week, a small family event with a few friends. Ainsley, it will be a special pleasure if you can join us."

"Are you are sure I would not be an intrusion . . ."

Logan urged, "I'm a newcomer to this family as well and you can be assured they are genuine and kind folk. For Flaxie's sake, please accept the invitation."

After Willoughby's team left Mont Blanc, Bernard's and Ingrid's focus shifted to the arrangements for Flaxie's party.

Ingrid was subtle with Logan. "It's been a whirlwind of activity since you arrived and you might think there is no end. If fate had not brought you here, you could not have stolen Flaxie's heart, and I would not now be married to my love.

"Recently I found Flaxie exploring her mother's jewelry, captivated by the exquisite diamond that her father had given to her mother. As it means the world to her, perhaps it could be a shared joy with Bernard's blessing if you had it reset.

"Monsieur Frobisher in the village designed the original setting and is a fine goldsmith and a family friend. Frederick and Francesca were very much in love like the two of you.

"My intention is not to pry or make an awkward suggestion, but I've been known to have excellent intuition."

She kissed Logan on the cheek.

"You are an extraordinary woman, Ingrid!"

The sunroom was being transformed for the event into a menagerie of balloons and colorful Gerbera daisies. Bernard spotted Ingrid across the room, teetering on a stepladder, hanging a 'Happy 25th Birthday' banner over the archway.

"Darling, you shouldn't be up there—a fellow from the concierge can do that."

Reaching up, he teased her like a schoolboy in love. "I have a good mind to sweep you off your feet and carry you away,"

"Bernard, I've always done these things. If you want to help, call Juliette and ask her to bring the cake. I had it specially made in three tiers. The base layer is the first eight years of her life with her parents, the second represents her growing years at the Grand, and the third is for her future and her own family. Numbered rosettes are on each year.

"And no it's not too fruffy, I put a lot of thought into it. Bernard, while you're downstairs, could you call the photographer from our wedding, I'd like a family portrait taken as Ainsley will be here."

"Of course, he'll be here."

"Bernard, it's what's best for Flaxie."

29

The Promise

On the uphill hike from the village, Logan stopped to take extra pleasure in the scenery and breathe in the fresh air. His hand went to his pocket to the ring. He had added two small diamonds encrusted around Frobisher's new gold setting of the Marceau heart-shaped diamond.

He pondered his proposal and in the exhilaration, he rose on his toes, as if he could run forever to burn off this energy.

Thinking only of Flaxie, he'd forgotten to watch his way and bumped square into Ainsley on the footpath.

"Hey pal, what are you doing here?" Logan asked.

"To the village to fetch Flaxie's birthday present."

"You could have borrowed the Vulcan."

Ainsley shrugged. "No, I am an independent sort. Perhaps I'll get the cog back later. Logan, I'm glad you encouraged me to go to the birthday party. I am delighted to find my sister after all these years. She is my only blood relative. You can't imagine how precious that is."

"Flaxie wants a future that includes you—she is counting on that. Make sure you stay close and don't go off and leave as it would break her heart."

"Why do you insinuate that?"

"Although you are working with the ranger unit as you paint, in time you will want more in life. If you believe your destiny is here, then tell Flaxie outright now. We are reviewing confidential matters, and I'm sure if you showed an interest in getting involved one way or another the family could find a place for you."

Logan saw a spark in Ainsley's eyes.

"I once read a humorous Leacock story about a cousin that over-stayed his welcome. It was painful in the end and I couldn't bear for the Marceaus to think of me in that way."

"I don't know that story, but openness and honesty are the best practices. You'll find your place."

After the last seating in the dining room, Ingrid Flaxie collected from the penthouse. "Come right now, dear, your birthday celebration is coming alive downstairs."

Logan was jittery in his euphoria as he watched her at the entrance. She walked slowly toward him and melted into his arms, then brushed her lips over his until he couldn't bear any more.

"Oooh! You'll have to wait until you get married, Logan," Marianne jeered, unaware that she was only baiting him.

He looked at Marianne, then Bernard and Ingrid, then back to Flaxie. Taking both of her hands, he went down on one knee and felt her tremble.

"Flaxie, you are everything to me. There's no one I would rather spend the rest of my life with than you. Will you marry me?"

"Yes, yes, yes, of course, I will." He placed the diamond on her finger. "It's perfect, Logan. I couldn't imagine anything more endearing than this."

Ainsley came through the door struggling with a large package, five feet by five feet, wrapped in brown paper.

He had missed the excitement and the crowd was still buzzing. At his entrance, someone gasped, "What on earth is that?" Others whispered, "Who is it?"

Ainsley knew that all eyes were following him. As the room quietened, he set the object against the wall and turned to face them.

"I'd like to explain my reason for being here, to the Marceau family in particular. You need to know the truth. I am the son of Francesca Stanhope.

"When I arrived in Paris I was disgruntled to hear that the great Chef Marceau was in town to add to his accolades. You see, I grew up in relative poverty. When my mother told me her deathbed secret, I was angry that I had been denied the Marceau birthright, jealous that I was forgotten and abandoned.

"Then I researched the Grand Marceau and its owners and could not find a derogatory word to hold against anyone. Instead, I saw only articles and examples of kindness and generosity.

"My adoptive parents loved me and provided the best that they could. Something inside me yearned to see my sister and to have a life where I belonged, so I decided to come to Chamonix. I arrived a few days before Christmas Eve and with no place or anyone to take me in, I took a room at the hostel."

Flaxie's lip quivered as she listened to his agony.

"That night, the whole village was talking about the

rescue by a Grand Marceau team to the woodcutter's cabin, bringing Christmas to forgotten children. Any jealousy I thought I had was gone and instead, I longed to be a part."

His voice cracked. "Then on Christmas Eve, the hostel manager said we would have Christmas dinner, after all, not only the hostel but anyone with a need. He said the Wenceslas spirit of giving was coming to the village."

Ainsley called up Flaxie. "That night was the first time I saw you, my dear sister, and you too, Logan. I was speechless and I didn't dare to approach you. I can never repay what that meant to me, but I spent the last few weeks doing what I can do."

He pulled the papered object away from the wall. "Flaxie, this is for you for your birthday. Thank you for reaching out this Christmas."

Tearing the paper, Flaxie gasped and stepped back for the crowd to see a magnificent acrylic painting of the Grand Marceau, with the Alps and the woodcutter's cabin high on the hill.

He read out the brass plate at the bottom. "To my Sister Flaxie on her Birthday. A Wenceslas Christmas – Ainsley Stanhope-Hayhurst."

Responding to the room's applause, Flaxie said, "This is a thrill beyond what I can describe. Coincidentally, the other day I was in Chamonix looking up at the hotel. I stopped, wanting to capture the scene in my memory. This is it, Ainsley, it is so beautiful. Thank you. Together we'll build a sibling bond that will create new memories. I am very proud of you."

Bernard Marceau's voice was broken. "Young man, this is more meaningful than you can ever imagine. If I can obtain Flaxie's permission, I know exactly where it will hang."

A Wenceslas Christmas

The first wing of the Wenceslas Chateau opened the following Christmas, expanding the splendor and opulence of the Grand Marceau. Centered in the grand foyer was the painting by Ainsley Stanhope, the popular, new artist from Chamonix.

Display windows of the new promenade shops were glittering with lights, and inside the Stanhope Gallery, Logan was amused to find Flaxie and Ainsley together hanging paintings.

The two blond heads tilted together side by side, admiring the positioning of the paintings and discussing his color theory in one of the vibrant mountain scenes.

"The colors portray the power of the Alps," Flaxie said, and Ainsley finished her thought. ". . . And the magnificence of Mont Blanc."

As Ernesto unloaded shipping boxes from the delivery bay, Ainsley unsealed and moved goods to the counter.

"Our souvenir t-shirts!" he shouted. "These depict the Wenceslas Chateau and the great King Wenceslas himself. Souvenirs already fly out every time a bus comes up from the village. We're getting requests for the history of the Grand Marceau and questions about the Wenceslas adventure now that it's Christmas. We have become a unique tourist attraction."

Logan waved a magazine. "It's here, a review of the acclaimed artist in town and the announcement of the official grand opening of the Wenceslas Chateau. It's appropriate that we invite the guests of honor to our ribbon-cutting ceremony."

Flaxie laughed. "I know what you have in mind. The six months of Chiassons—April, May, June, December, and dad and mom, October and January. This year Santa will come to the woodcutter's family at Mont Blanc, and Bodine will bring them down for the Christmas Eve Show. I hope the girls won't be too overwhelmed, meeting the real Father Christmas."

Flaxie embraced her husband.

"We'll never forget the reasons we stand here today, Logan. Remember from the song, 'Ye who now will bless the poor shall yourselves find blessing'."

"We have found *our* blessing!"

The End

About the Author

Shirley Burton is a Canadian author in fiction genres, including suspense thrillers in the Thomas York Series, old-fashioned whodunit capers in Inspector Furnace Mysteries, and nostalgic, family-oriented Christmas stories. Journey on her historical fiction from France in the 1500s, and let your imagination take you on the inspiring fantasy adventure *Boy from Saint-Malo*.

Shirley's residence is in Niagara-on-the Lake, Ontario, and Calgary, Alberta.

"I've been privileged to explore the locations of my books, walking the characters' neighborhoods and streets. Research has taken me to Istanbul, France, Italy, Greece, London, Amsterdam, Brazil, California, New York, and Quebec.

"Join me in my 600-page historical fiction, *Homage: Chronicles of a Habitant*, that portrays ten generations of a typical family migrating from France to the New World, paralleling real-world events over 500 years.

"There comes a time in life to take the leap into writing. It's that time for me."

Shirley Burton

shirleyburtonbooks.com

Christmas Books by Shirley Burton

CLOCKMAKER'S CHRISTMAS

A nostalgic Christmas story for all ages. A mother of two small children travels from Manhattan to Heidelberg to resolve an estate. In the magical setting of the Castle and the Christmas markets, she is tempted into a whirlwind romance. With matchmaking charm, a clockmaker bestows unique gifts on the couple. A feel-good, old-fashioned Christmas.

THE WISH STORE

An inspiring Christmas story in charming Chimney Ridge, Vermont. Rudy Hancock's Emporium is the town's focal point, with toys and imagination. It becomes the town's wish store at Christmas, turning wishes into miracles and deeds. With a lad helping as an elf, Rudy and the townsfolk fulfill the wishes of a veteran, a musician, a widow, a young girl, and a wanderer, celebrating at the Fezziwig Ball.

A WENCESLAS CHRISTMAS

A Christmas story of love and charity in the French Alps near Chamonix at a centuries-old luxury hotel. Chef Marceau's niece catches the eye of the sous-chef, sparking a romance. Following an avalanche and a family isolated in the mountains, a spirit of charity grows at the hotel, inspired by tales of the Good King Wenceslas. Together, the employees and guests carry the Wenceslas spirit into the village.

CHRISTMAS TREASURE BOX

Polly Perkins operates the family antique shop. In the days before Christmas, she finds her grandmother's diaries, revealing a lost love she had held from others in her life. Polly meets a man who whisks her into a romance. A distant relative claims on the family's resources, and Polly pursues a resolution toward a memorable Christmas Day.

Suspense Thrillers by Shirley Burton

DON'T OPEN THE DOOR

A thought-provoking suspense thriller. The romantic tension between Tess and her husband turns into a vacuum as she follows his advice for a shopping day in Manhattan, then disappears. She finds herself in the shopping district, but two years have passed without her knowledge. Detective Mitchell uncovers the past lives of Tess, Deane, and others, exposing a criminal connection that threatens Tess.

UNDER THE ASHES

Book One of THE THOMAS YORK SERIES. Debut suspense thriller in upstate New York begins with a high-speed chase that leaves the protagonist barely alive and his unknown passenger dead. Daniel Boisvert recovers from injuries, remembering nothing before the moment a train slammed into his car. He soon begins to suspect that the name he's been using may not be his own.

THE FRIZON

Book Two of THE THOMAS YORK SERIES. In a plot to steal great artworks from museums, a trio of rogues accumulates stolen works until a mysterious shadow recruits our series protagonists, Thomas and Rachel, to infiltrate a forgery scheme in Paris that is wreaking havoc on the art world. A thriller in the art community at Montmartre, Paris.

ROGUE COURIER

Book Three of THE THOMAS YORK SERIES. A client with suspicious motives recruits Thomas and Rachel in Paris to find her spouse, a courier gone missing. The trail of clues leads to London and Amsterdam to a ring of diamond thieves. The courier turns the tables, and a double-twist seals the couple's fate.

Suspense Thrillers by Shirley Burton

SECRET CACHE

Book Four of THE THOMAS YORK SERIES. A young man vacationing in Brazil is kidnapped and conned into participating in a bank robbery. Years later, one of the captured thieves set on revenge seeks the cash booty taken, leading him to a California vineyard with a connection. Thomas and Rachel race from Paris to Napa Valley to assist in a murder investigation of her Uncle Zach.

THE PARIS NETWORK

Book Five of THE THOMAS YORK SERIES. The young protagonists, Thomas and Rachel, are back in Paris. After the Bataclan terrorist attack, an encounter at the Basilica in Montmartre sets them on the track of a terrorist plot to collapse the catacomb system in Paris with a drone scheme. A former Interpol agent comes to their aid when Rachel's life is at risk. A contemporary story of terror and suspense.

THE MASQUERADE

Book Six of THE THOMAS YORK SERIES, in Paris. Thomas and Rachel receive an invitation to the French palace's annual costumed ball to diffuse a ransom heist to secure Napoleon artifacts tied to museum criminals. But all is not as it seems as they return to the events and culprits of an unsolved Paris scaffold heist from seven years before.

RED JACKAL

A thriller in Istanbul and on a Mediterranean cruise. Finn receives a letter from an Afghanistan war comrade, enticing him to retrieve an Ottoman artifact stolen from a Sultan's tomb. He infiltrates a smuggling ring to flush out the criminals. Double agents keep him on the run with the attractive Nicole Colbert, and he'd do anything to save her.

Mysteries by Shirley Burton

EPITAPH OF AN IMPOSTER

A suspense mystery with an imposter, a blackmailer, and unscrupulous members of the House of Lords. The astute collector of rare books in London comes upon an incriminating set of post-war journals of stuffy Lord Tannahill, with secrets of past crimes and of an imposter who crept into the Tannahill family. The bookseller conspires with an employee to expose a blackmail plot, as the drama intertwines past generations linked to an old English manor.

SENTINEL IN THE MOORS

A warm, comical vengeance in a charming setting. A museum archivist, Gabe Farrow, takes a sabbatical at a seaside village, Staithes, in England's North Yorkshire Moors. He discovers a plot to steal a hoard of Viking treasures in the moors. As he befriends the colorful townsfolk, his landlady and a young lad assist him in exposing the plot, testing the village's loyalty.

MYSTERY AT GREY STOKES

An Inspector Furnace Mystery, an old-fashioned whodunit. In an English country manor during Christmas festivities, guests arrive for a splendid feast. The cast includes the butler, housekeeper, the Berwick family members, and social guests. Inspector Furnace and Detective Prentice are called to the manor to untangle the deception and solve the case.

SWINDLE: MYSTERY AT SEA

An Inspector Furnace Mystery whodunit. The Inspector and his bride set out on a sailing on the Queen Elizabeth to New York. A body is found in the cargo, and as Inspector Furnace takes charge, a host of passengers and celebrities become suspects and amateur detectives at the nightly Captain's Table dinner to analyze clues and reveal the culprit.

Historical Fiction by Shirley Burton

HOMAGE: CHRONICLES OF A HABITANT

The ten-generation historical fiction begins in France in the 1500s. A 500-year journey based on a family's lives, tragedies, and immigration to North America. Experience typical life as the early migrants travel from France to settle in Quebec, with generational conflicts and cultural clashes in the new land. Share the joys and experiences of the immigrants, paralleled with researched historical events.

Fantasy Adventure by Shirley Burton

BOY FROM SAINT-MALO

An orphaned boy in explorer Jacques Cartier's hometown dreams of being a mariner. Young Gaeten enters a magical world of visionaries and inventors that guide him on his life's adventure. Sailing to the new world in the crow's nest on Cartier's ship begins an unbounded future. This story's theme can inspire all ages to live with a belief in oneself and without barriers.

Books are available online and can be ordered through bookstores in Canada, USA, UK, Europe, Australia, New Zealand, Asia, and South America

shirleyburtonbooks.com

CPSIA information can be obtained
at www.ICGtesting.com
Printed in the USA
BVHW040633070822
643857BV00001B/15